ANOMALY

A NOVEL

John L Owens

Author of *THE NINTH GENERATION*

This story is dedicated to those

who have awakened

in a world far from home.

1

GREEN PORT BEACH, FLORIDA—

Joel Landon never missed his morning beach run, even with a category-four hurricane lashing the shore. The storm's eye was now forty miles out, moving northeast. Joel was pumping south, energized by the wind. Churning waves tossed glistening foam across his path as runoffs cut through the sand. He loved where he lived, the rhythmic sounds of the sea, the salty smell of the air, and the crunch of shells beneath his feet. Nature's own workout gym, less the crowds.

Close to his usual turn-around, he thought he heard a female voice, but saw no one, just the cloudy seascape to the south, bending palms and water-streaked dunes to the west.

"Midnight." Her cry came again.

Joel slowed his pace and rounded a tall dune, then suddenly stopped–There stood a slim gray figure, slightly over five feet in stature, looking away.

"Midni–" She turned and faced Joel, her hand reaching into a waist pouch. "Keep your distance!"

Joel lifted both arms.

Her hand withdrew and tossed back the hood of her fitness suit revealing a familiar face and brown shoulder-length hair flowing in the wind. "Isn't your name Joel?"

"Amber?" He had seen her a few times at the weekly recovery meetings.

"Thank God."

"You were going to shoot me?"

"Just a defense trick I saw on TV."

"So, what's with Midnight?"

"My black lab. He ran ahead of me somewhere into the dunes."

"Didn't see him earlier but let me help you look." The powerful hurricane was eroding the coast on its pathway north, opening new sands.

"Midnight likes to explore. What are you doing here?"

"I've got a place just up the beach."

"I didn't know there were any homes in this area."

"No regular homes."

"Don't say it. You're the boat guy."

"My reputation must get around." Joel led the search through the inner dunes. "What brings you to my beach?"

"Oh, it's your beach?" Amber had an attractive smile.

"Not really, but I like to meet those who visit."

"Fair enough. We recently moved into a rental trailer at Oceanside RV Park – less expensive than an apartment, and right on the beach."

"We?"

"Me and my rescue dog, Midnight." Amber walked along with Joel while looking in all directions.

"Are you a dog lover?"

"An animal lover. It helps in my work."

"Your work, as a veterinarian?"

"Not me. I assist the Doctor at Beaches Animal Clinic." Amber stopped. "Wait. I hear Midnight."

Following the excited bark, they ran, finally spotting some movement through the sea oats near the bottom of a huge dune.

"Midnight?" Amber called, continuing to move closer. The dog was frantically occupied, fixed to its spot.

Water run-off from the higher inland elevation had eroded a sharp trench through the center of the dune, and it was at its base that the dog was digging furiously. Heaps of sand had been moved, exposing a long bony object.

"What have you found now?" Amber pulled a leash from the open pouch at her waist. "Midnight! Come!" She went to the animal and attached it. The dog yielded to her tug, still barking and growling as Amber restrained him.

Joel followed her gaze to the exposed area.

A well-preserved, massive fish skeleton at least six feet long lay unearthed, stretching from its fluked tail down toward the sea. He figured that it had been buried for a long time. "Some fish," breathed Joel.

Amber edged closer while shortening the leash on Midnight. "Those appendages on the sides don't look like fish fins."

Joel stepped forward to inspect the fish, fossil, or whatever it was. What she said was true. Two opposite sets of bones stretched from the upper part of the skeleton outward from each side, like… "arms?"

"Sea cows or dugongs have arm-like appendages," said Amber.

Joel grabbed a piece of driftwood and pushed it into the dirt just below one of the unusual bones and slowly levered it up. What appeared connected was a shock - a splay of finger-like bones. "Do sea cows have appendages like these?"

At first Amber was silent, still intently studying the mysterious remains while trying to keep Midnight away. "Can you get the head up?"

Joel brushed the end with his stick exposing a large rounded bone. He then started to lift. At first it held tight, then something snapped and up it popped. Joel stepped back.

"If I didn't know better…" Amber couldn't complete the sentence.

Joel was also at a loss for words. Such things didn't exist. He slowly scanned the skeleton – the distinct fluked tail and fish-like lower body. Then above a pelvic area, the spine and rib cage, arms, neck and skull– almost half-human, except for one thing. "There's no jaw," he said.

Amber was pointing to a pile of dirt not three feet from the head. "What's that?"

Joel saw a protruding bone that Midnight was sniffing, stepped closer, and slowly worked it free from the pile. He could feel his heart thump. "What is it?"

Midnight responded with another bark as Amber knelt for a better look. "Sit!" Finally, the dog obeyed her command.

Joel ran a finger over the large dark teeth. There were two rows with a few broken off and missing. The width of the jaw was over a foot. "He may have found a primitive shark. They have double rows." What does the Doctor's Assistant think?"

"We don't work on sharks, but if this is from one, a lot has changed. The teeth look freakishly human. And the structure of the mandible... It seems to match the skull."

"Sheepshead fish have human-looking teeth, and several rows," Joel spoke, hoping for something explainable.

"So do the Pacu, an invasive species from the Amazon, but none are this size." Amber picked the jawbone up and turned it. "The center front of the arch is thickened and buttressed. If this thing is a fish, it's the first one I've seen with a chin. Should we call someone?"

Joel pictured the local Sheriff at the scene scratching his head and having his deputy bag it and dispose of it to avoid the possibility of a weird news event.

"Like the D.N.R.?" suggested Amber, still fixed on the fossil.

Joel wasn't sure what the Department of Natural Resources would do with it, other than remove it and bump the responsibility for categorizing it on up the chain of command until a decision was ultimately forced on someone to label it or get rid of it. He had grown up in a military family and had heard how the government worked.

Another thought came to him — "Maybe we should just wait and see what we can learn about it. It's not going to swim off. I might even do an article on it along with some photos to document its existence."

"The veterinarian I work for seems to know a lot about all kinds of animals based on their bone structure. He has quite a collection. If you like, I can take the jawbone to him this afternoon and let him look at it." Amber was snapping a picture.

"That sounds like a plan." Joel withdrew his camera-phone from his pocket and took some shots from different angles including the jaw.

Amber unfolded a plastic tote bag while Joel picked up the jawbone and carefully slid it inside. After exchanging phone numbers, they parted company.

On his way back, Joel was still processing all that had happened with a mixture of excitement and uncertainty.

Back in his boat house, seated at his writing desk with a fresh cup of coffee, Joel reviewed the photos before speed-dialing the Beaches News editor, Stuart Glover. He liked working with Stu, an older slightly bald father-figure in his fifties who ran the paper like a Navy captain in a daysailer. Joel could tell that Stu wanted more. This morning he must have been waiting for a call —

"So, how's progress on the lagoon article?" Stu had mentioned it more than once, the idea of featuring the homes and lifestyles of the wealthy with waterfront lagoon property.

"Maybe a month away. Still need more material. A few dinner invitations wouldn't hurt."

"Any fresh ideas for our next issue?"

"Actually, I may have one." Joel paused, wondering what the best way might be to present the topic. "It's unusual."

"We can use unusual."

"This is something I found today, on the beach, exposed by the storm." Joel could hear Stu breathing. "A most unusual marine fossil."

"Some kind of fish?"

Joel hesitated, wanting to sound objective as a good reporter should. "It does have a fish-like tail, but the upper body is not like any fish you've ever seen."

There was silence.

"Stu, have you ever imagined what a mermaid might look like fossilized?" Even as the words came out, a nervous lump formed in his throat.

"A what?"

"I know how it sounds– "

"Have you stopped going to your meetings?"

"Trust me, I'm still going every week."

"My boy, I have no idea what you're talking about, but I've got some news you've been waiting for."

Joel sat up straight. "You got it, didn't you?"

"I did indeed. Turns out Lucas Redding is vacationing here for a few days. I've set up an interview with him for 7 PM this evening. Can you handle it?"

"Yes!" Joel pumped the air with his fist. He'd been trying to line up an appointment with the famed, but recluse, geneticist for weeks.

Amber arrived fifteen minutes early for work at Beaches Animal Clinic, her shift starting at 1pm. She had learned the rewards of punctuality and good work habits on her own, not from her upbringing by parents who drank to excess and gambled away their earnings. By working double jobs and hard study, she had managed to put herself through Junior College. Her excellent volunteer work at the animal rescue center earned her a rewarding job as an assistant at the clinic. Her experience with an alcoholic family also led her to attend the local AA meetings, but purely as support for those struggling. She had kept her vow to never touch the stuff.

Veterinarian, Dr. Leslie Lane, had already opened the clinic and was in his office reviewing the schedule for the day. A tap on his open door caused him to look up.

"Good morning, Amber. I would like for you to inventory our medications first; then I'll need your help with a couple of routine surgeries and a tracking chip implant."

"Right away." Amber was pleased to be trusted with greater responsibilities, not that she was above the menial tasks. She would do whatever was needed. But she had earned favor and she had one to ask of her boss, which she quickly slipped in. "Do you think that you might have a few minutes later to look at a jawbone fossil?"

"Sure. Did you bring it in?"

Amber lifted the bag. "Yes sir."

"Put it on the table. I'll have a look during our afternoon break."

It was shortly after 4 PM when break time came. Aside from being a good local veterinarian, Dr. Lane was an authority on animal bones. The evidence was apparent within the glass cabinets flanking his office walls. Bone samples, microscopes, exploratory tools and instruments were within easy reach as were volumes of reference books on the paleontology of modern and ancient animals.

The veterinarian cleared a place on his desk as Amber brought over the bag. She felt that some introduction was needed but decided not to say too much. After all he was the authority.

She reached in and slowly pulled out the wide jawbone setting it directly in front of him. "We found this on the beach and are not sure what it is."

The fossil had his full attention. He blinked several times, picked it up and turned it to different angles without saying a word.

"It's certainly unusual," said Amber, filling the silence.

A look of amazement spread across Dr. Lane's face. His eyes were fixed on the object as his fingers moved along the ragged double rows of teeth. They were dark and stone hard from mineralization.

After an awkward gap of time, Amber spoke again, "Do you have any idea what it might be, Dr. Lane?"

Without looking up, he finally spoke. "I would like to hold onto this for further examination...with your permission, of course." His expression was intense and had not lightened since his first glance.

It was not the time or place to say no. "That will be fine. I'll tell Joel that you've decided to keep it overnight."

"Joel?"

"Yes sir, he helped me find it, along with Midnight."

"Nearby?"

"Between our houses...that is, my trailer and his boat-home."

"Hmmm. Were there other bones that you noticed around it?"

Amber swallowed.

Dr. Lane shifted his penetrating gaze from the jawbone to Amber. "If you want my help, I need all the information you have."

"Just a quick photo."

"Can I see?"

Amber reached into her pocket and pulled out her camera phone. Locating the image and enlarging it on the screen, she showed it to the doctor.

Somewhat surprising her, he took it from her hand and quickly punched in some keys on the keypad. "Hope you don't mind if I send myself a copy." It was not really a question.

He then handed the phone back with a narrow smile. "You were going to do some cleaning up?"

Amber slowly backed out of the office. She hoped that Joel would understand.

A short interview had been arranged at 7 PM in the Donnelly estate for Joel with the distinguished geneticist, Dr. Lucas Redding. His editor, Stu, 20 years his senior, had described it as a rare opportunity which he did not want to let slide; so Joel had investigated the geneticist and prepared a few questions, hoping to get some quotes that might be a boost to the readership of The Beaches News. At the same time, if he handled it right, he could get an invitation back for an article on lagoon life among the affluent.

The heavy ornate door at 99 Lagoon Way creaked open, and a neatly collared face appeared inside.

"Joel Landon here, Beaches News."

"Ah yes, do come in," said the butler.

Joel was escorted through several rooms, down a hallway, to another door which the servant lightly rapped.

"Who is it?" a voice bellowed from inside the room.

"Your interview, sir, from The Beaches News," said the butler before leaving.

Joel stood there a minute until he saw the handle turn and the door swing inward.

"Let's get it over with," came the voice again.

Accepting that as his entry cue, Joel stepped into the room. "My privilege to finally meet the famous Dr. Lucas Redding." A man's name was always a good place to begin. Joel tried to look friendly but was slightly unnerved by the imposing dark countenance of this one.

"Do you care for a drink?" the doctor asked.

Joel wondered if a drink might help before replying, "No, thank you." There was no need to tempt his addiction.

A scotch glass in hand, Redding gestured to a soft chair. "Have a seat." Before the doctor sat, he scooped up a stack of papers from a table and pushed them out of sight. "I did agree to an interview but let's make it brief. As you must realize I have work to do."

"Of course," Joel replied, not sensing any comfort. "I just have a few questions, and we at the News certainly appreciate your time." Joel opened his tablet. "Can we start with a favorite genetic topic, dinosaurs?"

"Jurassic Park is not one of my projects. That's for Hollywood."

"Yes, but with the discovery of soft dinosaur tissue, do you think there's a possibility of replicating their DNA?"

"As I said, that's Hollywood nonsense. Such findings are highly questionable considering the evolutionary time frame of 65 million years."

"How could blood cells survive for so long encased in porous sandstone?"

"Those findings are under investigation."

"Investigation?"

"By respected mainstream scientists. Let's move on to something else."

Joel had hoped to get more information from Redding on the T-Rex blood vessels, having studied the data from several sources, but seeing no way, decided to jump in with Stu's big question.

How was he going to explain the interview to Stu? He had made Joel's lifestyle possible by letting him fix up an abandoned boat that was left in the dunes and live in it on his property. In return Joel cranked out a weekly article for The Beaches News which Stu owned and published. They had a good relationship which had grown stronger in the three years since Joel had wandered into town, not long out of college. Further thoughts and scribbling filled a few hours until sack time arrived, then he pulled himself up the ladder to his sleeping quarters.

The topside cabin of the old shrimp boat was the pilot house. A corner shower and head had been added plus some shelving and a dresser, but the original wheel with magnetic compass was still in place. Windows encircled the cabin providing a great daytime view of the coast. An aft door provided access to the open fantail deck, with chairs and round table, an ideal spot for morning coffee with the sunrise.

Joel closed his eyes as he stretched out on his bed. With much on his mind, he finally surrendered to sleep. For how long he wasn't sure. At first it seemed like a dream, until it all got closer and louder. He was not imagining it. There was the distinct whup, whup, whup of helicopter rotors and circling beams of light. He sat up suddenly and looked at the clock. This was not the kind of activity to visit Green Port, especially at 2 AM. He got up from bed and went to the ocean-side windows.

At least two aerial units could be seen scouring the beach while traveling north to south. They looked like special ops military helicopters, powerful light beams streaming from each, searching and circling again. What on earth were they looking for? Then other sounds of movement – a vehicle engine, metal doors and voices could be heard to the south. Joel stepped out onto the fantail deck to try to see what was happening.

In the distance to the south, Joel could see lights and movement on the beach. The helicopters were hovering and training their lights on one area. Almost too late, he grabbed the binoculars from inside. He focused and watched as a large boat-shaped vehicle with tank-like wheels opened its rear doors. Then men in camouflage, six that he counted, slowly loaded a long box, the size of a casket. Joel's stomach felt as though a hand had reached into his abdomen and squeezed. It was the same spot in the dunes that he and Amber had made their unusual fossil find.

Joel rushed back inside, picked up his cell phone, and punched 911. There was no ring. Then he noticed there was no signal, strange since he had never lost his signal there before. He then hit the light switch. There was no power.

His next response was to investigate. Running his hand alongside the door, he located the halogen flashlight kept there for emergencies. With the light he located the clothes he quickly needed and made his way down the rear steps and onto the beach. The noises had ceased. There was just the soft pounding and sloshing of the surf and the rustling wind in the trees. Except for Joel's light everything was dark. No signs of activity.

It didn't take long to get to the location. Sweeping his light as he walked, Joel soon spotted a pair of wide tractor trails coming from the water's edge, as from an amphibious vehicle. He followed them back toward the dunes until they disappeared. With the rising tide those impressions would be washed smooth before the light of day.

Continuing back to the huge dune, Joel followed his flashlight, searching for any evidence of what had just occurred. There were no tracks, no footsteps, nothing.

Whatever had been there was now gone. Raked clean. The site of the skeleton had been completely altered. There was no hole or depression. Even the deep erosion on the side of the massive dune had been filled in and brushed over. Along with the tightness in the pit of his stomach, a strange chill ran up his spine as Joel turned to walk back to his place.

"Joel Landon reporting in at 8:30 AM? This is a surprise." Stuart Glover looked up from his makeshift desk at the back of his paper-stacked office. The smell of newsprint was as strong as the coffee, still perking. "Have a cup."

"Thanks." Joel helped himself, then pulled up a folding chair directly in front of Stu. "Guess you've heard."

"The interview?"

"Not much of one."

"Fill me in."

"Everything's highly classified." Joel met Stu's gaze and took a sip.

"That's it?"

"I gave it my best shot. Had a lot of questions, but he wouldn't open up. Even for The Beaches News."

"Did he say anything about his reason for coming to Green Port?"

"You said it was a vacation."

"That's what I heard but wasn't sure." Stu thumped his desk with his pencil.

"I did manage to irritate him."

The owner-editor blinked twice. "Doctor Lucas Redding, perhaps the world's leading geneticist and military advisor, is upset with us?"

"Nothing serious. Just a question he didn't like."

"What kind of question?"

"How DNA could have evolved by itself over time."
Stu looked puzzled.

"He said it didn't, and that other leading scientists agreed."

"So how does he think life happened?"

"That it was seeded."

"How?"

"That's when it got a little crazy and I had to leave."

The expression on Stu's face appeared more fatherly than editorial. "Do we owe the Doctor an apology?"

"For asking a question?"

Stu was silent, pressing the pencil to his chin. "I'm sorry the interview bombed," said Joel, "but we may have something much bigger to report."

"Bigger than Redding?" Stu cocked an eyebrow.

"How about this for a heading: Covert beach invasion takes fossil and returns to sea."

Stu tilted his head backward, eyes rolling.

"Seriously. Listen to me, Stu. I woke up at 2 AM to the sound of helicopters over our beach. Surely someone else must have heard something."

Deep furrows were forming in Stu's brow.

Joel continued, "They were circling with searchlights. I went outside and watched from my deck as they found what they were looking for, just south in the dunes."

And what were they looking for?"

"The very skeleton I mentioned earlier."

"Oh, yeah. The mermaid." Stu was forcing a smile.

"Stu, I know what you're thinking, and I have not relapsed. I haven't touched a drink, though Dr. Redding did offer me one."

"So, tell me, Joel, what happened when they found this skeleton?"

"They loaded it into an amphibious vehicle and disappeared into the sea."

"A great story, I will admit. Of course, you have some way to corroborate it." It was evident that Stu didn't believe a word of it.

"Uh, well, I went to check the area; but they had emoved and covered everything. Tracks washed clean by e tide."

"No pictures? Nothing?"

Joel paused, then remembered – "Wait." There were pictures of the skeleton he and Amber had taken. them up on his camera-phone, Joel showed them

anned the few photos briefly and handed it back. more than this."

is something more."

hat?"

one. We still have it."

nore later."

and goldies from your beaches music 'd your hand' – click."

owed 10:15AM as Amber wheeled er usual space at work, despite the e was no work for her today, or

n one she recognized, and she hat was going on. Her reason k up the fossil bone she had amine. There should be no d to Joel.

he front reception area, a new red-headed girl t the furry patient. ally, I work here." n being trained."

"No problem, I just need to see Dr. Lane." Amber saw no need to ask permission and decided to move past the new girl to the offices in the back.

"I'm Barbara."

"Hi Barbara. Amber. Nice to meet you." As she spoke, she noticed Barbara's hand go for the inter-office phone, but continued to walk into the hall and to the Veterinarian's office.

Amber had barely tapped when the door swung open.

"Amber, what brings you here? Did you not receive our call?" There was an unusual agitation in the doctor's face.

"Yes, I got somebody's call, but I didn't think you would mind if I came by to pick up that bone fossil."

"Of course, that one you wanted me to analyze." The doctor was making no room in the doorway for Amber enter. Rather, he was pulling on his coat, as if leaving. "N to belittle your discovery," he continued, "but I would get too excited. The bone appears to be nothing more that of a sea cow."

Amber was not too surprised by the report a backed up a little. "What do you make of the picture arm-like appendages?"

"An anomaly, just a genetic variation, but sti cow – please excuse me." He was pulling his offi closed behind him. "I'm already late for a meeting be glad to dispose of it for you later."

"Actually, I need to return it to – "

"You'll have to check back with me later, last words Amber heard as the doctor breezed

Dr. Lane was driving away as Amber left th headed back to her car. However, before turr she pulled out her phone and punched in the had given her.

He was quick to answer. "Amber, I've been trying to reach you. We've got to talk."

"Sorry, my phone's been off."

"It's okay. Where are you?"

"At the clinic."

"Did you get the bone back?"

"Not yet. The veterinarian had a meeting to attend."

"Where is it?"

"Still here, in Doctor Lane's office, I think."

"We have to get it."

"Joel, there's no need. He said it's only a sea cow."

"Amber, believe me. The doctor is either mistaken or lying."

"How can you say that?"

"Because of what happened on our beach at 2 AM. I'll explain later, but the skeleton was taken."

"Taken by who?"

"I can't explain now. But please listen. If there is any way you can get it back quickly, we need to get it."

"I'll call you back within thirty minutes."

Barbara was still at her post, peering over the counter. "Still no dog?"

"Left him at home. Remember? I work here."

The redhead showed a slight look of embarrassment as Amber moved past her.

"It's all right, Barbara. I just need to pick up something I left earlier."

An eyebrow lifted.

"Dr. Lane knows about it. I'll be out in a minute." Amber kept walking toward the back office.

Nothing more was said.

Amber quietly let herself in and turned on the overhead light. She moved around quickly looking over the doctor's collection of fossil fragments and bones scattered among instruments for testing and examination, on shelves and in cabinets. Nothing looked like the jawbone.

This was not the sort of thing she felt comfortable doing. Her heart was racing considering the chance that the doctor might come back, finding her searching his office without authorization. She had to hurry.

It was taking too long. Amber was about to abandon her search, thinking it foolish to risk her job over a sea cow skeleton, when something in a base cabinet caught her eye. A sliding door was partly open and there it was – the jawbone and her bag.

Quickly retrieving it, she tucked it under her arm and turned off the light. Amber politely exited the building past Barbara. Not until she was back in her car and heading down the drive, did she fully let out her breath.

Why should she feel so nervous? Why did she feel guilty for simply getting something back that belonged to her, or rather to Joel? She could explain it later to Dr. Lane, at least that's what she told herself on the way home and it made her feel somewhat better. Her phone rang on the way.

It was Joel, "Did you get it?"

"Yes, I have it."

"Any problems?"

"Not really."

"That's good. Can you keep it till later, in an out- of-the-way spot?"

"Sure." Amber's rental trailer wasn't the roomiest place, but it did have a small utility storage closet in a back room.

"I'll pick you up in an hour."

"What did you say happened at 2AM?" Her curiosity was high.

"Just get home safely. I'll tell you more in person."

The Ming Sun Diner had a flashy sign advertising their buffet but few cars, which impressed Joel that the small family-owned restaurant could use some extra lunch business.

"Chinese?"

"Sounds good," replied Amber.

Inside, only two of the tables were occupied. They settled into a corner booth at the far end which offered the privacy Joel wanted for discussing recent events.

The second they were seated, strings of beads clattered, and a smiling oriental lady emerged from the nearby doorway with two menus in hand.

"I'm not very hungry," said Amber, looking first at Joel then up at the waitress. "Can I just get a spring roll and some wonton soup?"

"Most certainly," she said. "Would you like our special happy bowl?"

"Just a cup, please."

"Most certainly. And for you, sir?"

"The buffet," said Joel, managing a friendly American smile. "And some iced tea."

"Water for me," said Amber, gazing around at the ornate Chinese wall hangings and decorative trim surrounding a statue of Buddha.

It wasn't ten minutes before they were served, and Joel had helped himself to a plate of brown rice and General Tso's chicken.

"You must like spicy food."

"And you?"

"Every now and then," said Amber, as she read the description on her placemat. "Did you know it's the year of the dragon?"

"Ever wonder who comes up with stuff like that?"

Amber filled her spoon with soup, then set it down. "Can you tell me now?"

"I will but I'm not sure you'll believe me."

"Well, at least try me."

Joel finished his bite of food, took a sip of his drink, then looked Amber squarely in the eyes. "To begin with, I don't believe in mermaids, unicorns or dragons."

Amber said nothing.

"Whatever it was we found on the beach had to be some kind of fish," Joel continued, "so why anyone would've wanted it that bad, or how they even knew it was there, I can't explain."

"Joel, what are you talking about? What happened?"

Pushing his plate to the side, he proceeded to describe all the details he had observed, starting with the helicopters at 2 AM, and ending with the vanishing of the amphibious vehicle along with the skeleton.

Amber was silent, deep in thought.

"I can't blame you. Stu didn't believe it either. I do go to meetings and am a recovering alcoholic."

"I know, and I go to those meetings with you." Amber's gaze fell slightly. "Did you relapse?"

"No. I really didn't. I'm telling you the truth, what I saw with my own eyes."

"Well, if all that did happen, what do we do now?"

"All we have left are the pictures, for what they're worth, not very clear."

"And the jawbone," said Amber, "which Dr. Lane claims is from nothing but a sea cow."

"Must've been some sea cow, for a special forces unit to come and get it."

"Are you going to open your fortune cookie?" said Amber, tearing the wrapper from hers.

"Nah."

She unfolded the paper and raised her eyebrows, as she read, "You are wise to keep your plans secret."

3

"Mr. Landon, I have checked with the other officers on duty and none of them have any reports of unusual disturbances during that time period."

"Can you direct me to any other agencies that might have any knowledge of a government operation on our local beaches?"

"You said there were sounds like a helicopter and lights just south of your place?"

"That's right."

"At around 2 AM?"

"Loud enough to wake me up."

"There were a few thunderstorms reported in the area."

"It was no thunderstorm."

"Sir, you can be assured that if the state or federal government had something planned to involve our county beaches, we would know about it."

"So, there's no one else I can call?"

"I'm sorry we can't be of more help, Mr. Landon."

Joel called the nearest Search and Rescue office of the U.S. Coast Guard but met with a similar response from the junior officer on duty – nothing unusual in the area to report. No cases since the hurricane had passed.

Banging the desk-top with his fist, Joel decided to call his father, although it had been over two years since they had spoken.

"Senator Landon's office. How may I help you?" She sounded genuine.

"I need to speak to the Senator."

"They have been in session. Would you care to leave a message?"

"Just tell him Joel tried to reach him."

"Does he know you, Joel?"

"I'm his son."

"Oh, excuse me. Just a minute. Please wait."

...Click. "Joel? Is it you?" It was his father's distant but familiar voice.

"It's me."

"How have you been?"

"Better. How are things in Tallahassee?"

"The usual work. You know how it is. What do you need?"

"It's not money."

"I wasn't suggesting – "

"I know. I have a job and a place now."

"That's good to hear."

"I have a different kind of problem."

"Let me change phones," said the Senator. A short pause. "Is it a woman?"

"It's not that."

"Go ahead."

"Okay – this morning about 2 AM I woke up to the sound of helicopter rotors and saw spotlights from two choppers searching the beach here in Green Port. A little later I spotted a vehicle near the dunes, must've been amphibious, that disappeared into the ocean after getting what they came for."

"And that was?"

"A skeleton that looked like a mermaid," Joel spoke before he thought how his father might take it.

The Senator was silent.

"Well actually it was just a sea cow."

There was still silence.

"Okay. I don't know why they came, but whoever it was that invaded our beach left no trace they had ever come. Local law enforcement says they know nothing about it. Neither does the Coast Guard. I thought you might be able to find out something, if it's our government."

"No one else saw or heard what you are saying?"

"Well, there was a girl who saw the skeleton with me before it was taken."

"A girl?"

"A young woman that I met at our recovery meetings."

"I'm glad to hear that you're going. How are you doing?"

This time Joel was silent.

"Of course, I will look into that matter, but can't make any promises."

"I'm not asking for any." Joel closed the call and briefly closed his eyes before getting up to shake some turtle food into Murf's box.

Searching his camera photo file, Joel enlarged the three pictures he had taken of the beach skeleton, examining them one-by-one. Two were washed out by the poor contrast in the light sand. Only one had any distinguishable features. It was time for a follow-up with Stu, having sent it along with an idea for a write-up.

"I'm glad you called. I have no problem with you doing an article on the skeleton. Just keep it light. Our readers can use a little mermaid humor."

"Like the title, 'Manatee Mermaid'?"

"Don't get too cute. Just remember, we're showing how a beach tourist might mistake a sea-cow for a mermaid, just seeing the skeleton. Work it around the picture."

"You foul spirit. You afflicting devil. I command you to release this man and get out in the Name which is above every name, Jesus Christ!"

Simon Johnson watched as the upper torso of the truck-driver heaved, and the glaring eyes and tense facial countenance transformed into a peaceful expression with a long exhale. The earlier heaviness and anxiety now gone. Another prisoner set free.

"All I can say, man, is thanks."

Words could never fully express the joy Simon felt at such times. "All thanks go to Him, the One who made heaven and earth."

"I never knew stuff like that was real."

"Bruce, it's a world of invisible warfare and your soul is the prize."

The truck-driver looked down at his watch. "I'm on an electronic log and gotta go. Next time through I want to talk some more about all this."

"I understand. Let's pray and I'll give you some materials to take with you, something you can listen to on the road."

As soon as Bruce had left the mobile chapel to return to his rig, Simon arranged the chairs in a small circle to accommodate the members of a local recovery group. Their leader was sick, and someone had suggested they call Chaplain Simon Johnson at the Oasis Truckstop.

It was close to 6 PM when the group of three arrived. The modified 40-foot semi-trailer offered an ideal ministry setting for truck drivers with a nicely paneled interior and end room designed for a live-in chaplain.

"Sorry to hear that Robert is sick, but glad to have you drop in." Simon waited to make sure they were all seated and comfortable. "I don't have the recovery books here that you normally use, but we can use the Bible. Everyone okay with that?"

"Sure. It's the good book," said Al. You want us to start like we do in our meetings?"

"How's that?" Simon knew that the Alcoholics Anonymous organization had been started by Christians and was based on Biblical principles.

"My name is Al, and I'm an alcoholic."

"My name is Joel, and I'm an alcoholic."

"Hi. My name is Amber, and I'm here for support. My parents were alcoholics."

"Welcome to the Good News Chapel. My name is Simon, and it's good to have all of you here. Can we start with a short prayer?" Seeing all three heads bowed, he began, "Holy Father, you know our needs before we can say them. Have mercy upon us this evening and set us free. Free from all lies. Free from all bondages of the enemy. In Jesus Name. Amen."

"Since none of you seem to have brought one, let me offer you all a free Bible, compliments of Word Transport Ministries." Simon reached around and distributed the short stack of gift Bibles to the group.

After taking a few minutes to find out something about each of the people, Simon shared some of his own background and how he had wound up as a truck-stop chaplain after losing his teaching position at a state university.

Of the three visitors, Joel seemed to show the most interest. "Were you teaching the Bible in place of the college text?"

"That wasn't my intent. But it did have answers for some of the students' questions that the textbook lacked, which I offered to share after class."

"Someone must not have believed it," said Joel.

"There are those who would rather avoid the truth than admit what they have been teaching is a lie."

"That's messed up," said Al, "that they would fire you for telling the truth."

"Irrational hatred of the truth was what led to the crucifixion of Jesus, and such persecution is also prophesied to accompany His followers."

"My higher power shows me things through dreams," said Amber.

"Dreams can come from God." Simon paused, "And they can come from other sources."

"Like?"

"Well, Amber, dreams can come from our own minds; and our minds can be influenced by spirits, good and evil."

The group was silent.

"Did you know that the Bible says that alcoholics will not enter the kingdom of God?" said Simon.

"Are you serious?" said Al.

"This is talking about those who choose to stay drunk."

"No one is perfect," said Amber.

"There is One," said Simon, "and if any of you are joined to Him – Jesus Christ – by faith, you are declared a new creation. The old self-destructive life is passed away. Let's take the time to see the truth for yourselves in Galatians 5:21, and 2 Corinthians 5:17."

After reviewing the references, Al excused himself from the meeting, thanking the chaplain for his teaching. Although the meeting time was over, Joel and Amber remained.

"You seem to have a lot of answers," said Joel.

"Maybe a few," said Simon.

"In your studies have you ever come across the mention of mermaids in the Bible?"

"That's one I haven't heard before. Why do you ask?"

"We're just curious," said Amber.

Simon rubbed his brow, silently questioning God as to how to proceed. His eyes settled on the bookshelf containing a resource library at the front end of the chapel. "Before we see what the Bible says about that possibility, allow me to read you a brief description from an ancient medical doctor."

The chaplain walked over and pulled a book down from the top shelf. It was a worn paperback Penguin Classic, Pausanias Guide to Greece, Volume 1.

"Pausanius was a doctor from Greek Asia Minor who devoted many years to recording the details of every Greek city in mainland Greece in the brief golden age of the Roman Empire, the second century A.D."

As Simon turned the pages, Joel said, "And they had mermaids?", a tongue-in-cheek remark.

"Have you heard the term, triton?" asked Simon.

"Is that like a titan?" asked Amber.

"Possibly related in origin, but the triton came from the water." Simon had found the page. "Let me share this with you."

"Go on." Joel was ready to listen.

"The doctor claims to have seen more than one of these among the wonders of Rome. Here is his description:

'Tritons are certainly a sight; the hair on their heads is like the frogs in stagnant water: not only in its froggy color, but so sleek you could never separate one hair from the next: and the rest of their bodies are bristling with very fine scales like a rough-skinned shark. They have gills behind the ears and a human nose, but a very big mouth and the teeth of a wild beast. I thought the eyes were greenish-grey, and they have their hands and fingers and fingernails crusted like seashells. From the breast and belly down they have a dolphin's tail instead of feet.'"

"That's one report we never got in biology class," said Joel.

"Let me add, a modern footnote to this account reads, 'This admirable and primitive creature is unfortunately not yet known to marine scientists.'"

"That's putting it mildly," said Amber. "Today people would think you're crazy to believe that such a thing exists – I mean, might have existed."

"How true," said Simon, closing and returning the book to the shelf. "But there is also the Biblical record."

"You mean these things are described in the Bible?" asked Joel.

"Well, not precisely; but there is a strong clue to their origin in Genesis, if you have an interest in exploring it."

"A little later, maybe," said Joel. "I think we've learned enough for one night."

"Understood," said Simon. "You're always welcome to drop by. I don't pretend to have all the answers, but with God's help we can usually find what we need."

After a friendly departure of the last two guests, the chaplain sat still and reflected. The subject of mermaids had never been brought up before and it was puzzling as to how God might use such an unusual discussion, hopefully for good.

Amber appreciated the ride back from the meeting and was beginning to sense a growing bond between herself and this somewhat strange beach reporter. If all that he had said was true about the beach invasion, a deep mystery remained concerning the missing skeleton.

"An interesting fellow, the chaplain, don't you think?" said Joel, his hand resting on the wheel as they neared the RV park where Amber was staying.

"Not very tolerant toward those with alcohol dependency."

"Yeah. That part was certainly different, drunkards not going to heaven. Didn't know that was in the Bible."

"I don't think Simon is AA certified," said Amber. "At least he had some stuff on mermaids—tritons he called them. Is this your place?"

Amber gathered up her bag and the gift Bible that Simon had insisted she take. "This is the place and thanks for the ride." She loosened her seatbelt and stepped out.

"Take care," said Joel, as she closed the Jeep door.

They exchanged smiles as he pulled away.

The ocean breeze was rustling the palms as Amber readied her door keys under the yellow bug light. The handle lock released as she turned the key. She then inserted it into the dead bolt, but found it already unlocked. She needed to be more careful and remember to lock both locks. Stepping inside, Amber flipped on a light and tossed her things on the table.

"Midnight?" Usually the black lab was waiting at the door to greet her.

A low whine from the next room.

"What's wrong, boy? You okay?" When she went to look, she found her dog cowering in the corner.

Amber checked around, turning on more lights as she scanned the trailer for anything unusual. Nothing appeared out of place.

The thought of anyone breaking in had not been seriously considered as such concerns had never arisen or been reported among her near neighbors. The beachside RV park was a safe and friendly place, one reason she had picked it and settled in.

Midnight gradually returned to normal. Amber walked through the trailer once again, just to be sure, before getting ready for bed. There was one thing that made her a little nervous, unsure why. But she felt that she needed to check the small utility closet where she had placed the fossil. It was a small out-of-the-way door in the back room behind some furniture, not a place one would look for a closet.

Amber turned the latch and looked in. There it was.

A thump against the door caused Joel to set down his morning coffee. It was the weekly edition of The Beaches News the courier had tossed. Not really interested in seeing it, still disappointed in how his interview had turned out, he went out and picked it up and returned to his galley desk.

His eyes stopped halfway down on the front page— "RENOWN GENETIC SCIENTIST VISITS GREEN PORT."

Joel scanned the short article listing some of Dr. Lucas Redding's credentials and expressing his appreciation for the preservation of the area's natural beauty and local friendliness. It was pretty much as Joel had submitted, nothing to brag about. No real breaking news.

How he wished that Stu would give him the go-ahead to expose all that had happened surrounding the skeleton seizure, but he needed more to go on than a few blurry pictures and a bone. He had called various authorities, surely one of which should have known or heard something involving such an operation, but nothing. Even his father, a Florida Senator with government connections, had no further information when Joel had last checked.

As he sipped his coffee and turned the page, Joel suddenly stiffened. On page 3 were the two pictures he had sent to Stu of the skeleton and jawbone. They were linked to an article he had not written titled, "Manatee Mermaids Give Visitors a Thrill."

The article read, "Throughout ancient history sailors have reportedly been lured to their watery deaths by the siren calls of mermaids. Recently there has been a growing fascination with the topic and prospect of such creatures existing; however, scientists now generally agree that what has often been mistaken for a mermaid is an animal common to our southern waterways and occasionally the ocean, the sea cow or dugong.

"The similarities were recently brought home to us by a sighting of such a skeleton on our own beach in an undeveloped area of Green Port. One of our staff, Joel Landon, was able to photograph one of these before it washed back into the sea. Fortunately, it failed to lure Joel to his death as he continues to write for The Beaches News."

Stu answered Joel's call on the fifth ring, "Guess you noticed I was able to use your photos. Made for an interesting insert. Didn't think you'd mind the humor."

"It was a surprise."

"We were in a pinch and had to put something together. Hope you're okay with me writing it."

"Sure. But it's misleading."

"How?" said Stu.

"The skeleton didn't just wash back into the sea."

"Do you have any evidence that it disappeared any other way?"

Joel was silent, his stomach in knots.

"As a reporter you need to be thorough. I had DNR look at your photos. Like the article says, it's just a sea cow. A bit strange in places, but still a sea cow."

4

Maybe it was a manatee, Joel tried to reason. But it didn't explain all the trouble it took to secretly remove whatever it was from the beach. He was in a quandary. What more could he do to find someone who knew?

Two sharp raps at his door interrupted his thinking.

It was Amber with a bundle in her hands.

"Surprise," said Joel. "This has to be a good morning. Coffee?"

"Take it."

"And that is…"

"Your bone!"

Joel reached out as Amber almost threw it into his arms.

"I don't want any more to do with it."

"Can you at least come in? Can we talk about it?"

"I need some space, Mister Newsman. This is much more than I can handle right now." Her face and hair looked like she had just lost a pillow fight, not the self-assured appearance Amber usually projected.

"I'm sorry. If I knew– "

"How could you know that the jawbone of a manatee was going to keep me up all night with Midnight whining and barking?"

"This thing did that?"

"I finally put it in the car, and he quieted down. I just feel strange with it in my trailer."

"Again, I'm sorry."

"Maybe you'll have no problem with it, but I need some rest." Amber turned and was walking away.

"Can I give you a ride?"

"No thanks. I need a little time alone."

Joel slowly closed the door and set the bone bundle down in the corner. No sooner had he straightened up than the phone rang.

"Is this Joel Landon, reporter for The Beaches News?" It was a deep resonating voice, strangely familiar.

"You got him."

"Joel, is this a convenient time to talk?"

"As good as any. Do I know you?"

"We had a brief interview the other day. Lucas Redding."

Of all people to be calling him, why? Joel's mind was frantically racing, and no words were coming.

"I hope you don't mind. I obtained your number from Stuart Glover."

"Not at all–uh–Doctor Redding." Good old Stu could've at least given him a heads up.

"Lucas is fine. Say, I appreciate your kind write-up in the latest issue. The folks here at Green Port have been like family." Somehow the words didn't connect.

"I'm glad you liked it."

"I also enjoyed the article on your unusual discovery, and the photos."

"Right. The sea-cow."

"Or whatever it was." There was a slight question in Lucas's tone.

"The DNR identified it."

"Which you trust as accurate."

"Aren't they reliable?"

"Most of the time."

Joel was silent.

"The skeleton is gone?"

"Without a trace."

"And all that remains is a jawbone?"

"That's it."

"Are you satisfied with the results of the Department of Natural Resources photo analysis?"

Joel hesitated and Lucas continued, "As a genetic scientist I have many contacts. There are laboratories nearby that can do a DNA analysis. If you would like, I can arrange a full spectrum bone test that will leave no doubt as to what the animal was."

"I doubt that I can afford such a test."

"Joel, I admire your determination. And to help you resolve this matter, I am offering the service at no cost to you. Let's leave no stone unturned, as they say."

"That is what they say."

"So, can I make the arrangements for the analysis tomorrow?"

"How long will it take?"

"With our technology, about six hours."

"Okay. But I want to take it there."

"Of course. I will call you in the morning with the address. Get a good night's rest, Joel."

"You too—uh—Lucas."

Dr. Lucas Redding smiled as he pocketed his phone and poured himself a tall glass of his favorite Scotch, then lowered himself into the soft recliner alongside a computer console facing a giant screen monitor against the wall. He relished his powers and position, able to influence global decisions through the elite scientific group – the Jasons, of which he was a respected member, and of course DARPA and the Department of Defense which he occasionally advised. There were others.

This matter which had come up unexpectedly on the East Coast of Florida, where he happened to be, was indeed fortuitous and would be a proverbial feather in his cap. Tilting the glass to his lips, he savored the familiar spirits and half-closed his eyes.

Just then a noise diverted his attention to the side of the room. He knew what the sharp flap meant and turned his head in that direction just in time to see the dark emergence of a ten-foot tall black-winged creature. Once it had retracted its wings, it was human in appearance. Ugly and scarred, but like a man.

"Good evening, Dracor," said Lucas, setting his drink down on the table. "Can't you guys ever call before you show up?"

No reply was given, just an unsettling stare.

"At least you could come as an angel of light instead of like Batman. Isn't that within your powers?"

"Today's generation prefers the dark angels. It feels more natural."

"I see. So, what brings you here tonight?" "Our rulers."

"Not our Prince?"

"Lucifer has been advised."

"What's the concern? I have everything under control. We will have the jawbone by tomorrow without alarming any officials."

"No more mistakes."

"The photos were unknown until publication," said Lucas defensively.

"Our network is better than that."

"Well, somehow the photos slipped through." Lucas felt some satisfaction in being able to point out a weakness in the spirit world's intelligence gathering.

"The veterinarian did not divulge that part to the Smithsonian. But we are taking care of it now," said

Dracor, unfolding his wings. "Just keep in mind, the stupid reporter has a father who is a State Senator. This needs to be handled flawlessly."

"And it will be," said Lucas.

With another leather-like flap, Dracor was suddenly gone. And so was the Scotch.

Lucas picked up an aerosol can of room deodorizer and aimed it in the direction of his parting guest.

The prominent gold lettering on the face of the gray marble multi-wing building read,

"GLOBAL-TEK GENETIC TESTING, RESEARCH & DEVELOPMENT".

Joel had been GPS-guided to the Orlando complex by 9AM, following Lucan Redding's early call. The place had the feel of a hospital with a spacious entrance-reception area along with a medicinal smell. Swatches of abstract art gave some color to the otherwise bland commercial furnishings.

Joel trekked in with a bundle under his arm, past clusters of empty seating, all the way to the office window which revealed a human presence fully occupied with his desk work. The middle-aged slightly- bald man wore a wrinkled white shirt with a gray lab apron. He appeared startled to see someone at his window.

"Can I be of assistance to you?"

"Do you do DNA analysis here?"

"Paternal analysis? No."

"What about bones?"

Inching his glasses up his nose, he said, "What kind of bones?"

"If I knew that, I wouldn't be here."

"Of course. Global-Tek is one of the few laboratories that offers a full spectrum analysis, able to match genomes of every species of biological life."

"How fast can you analyze this?" Joel opened the package placing the jawbone on the counter in full view of the office window.

"A most interesting specimen," said the technician, standing for a better look. "You will need to fill out some papers."

"Did you receive a call from a Doctor Lucas Redding?"

Before he could reply, another male voice came from the office area, "Otis, you're needed in centrifuge, room four. I'll take care of Mr. Landon." As Otis departed, the one speaking came into view, a tall man in a business suit with an extended handshake. "Please overlook our assistant. We've been expecting you. All arrangements have been made. No paperwork is necessary."

Joel watched as the tall man gathered the packaging around the fossil and assumingly placed it on a table inside the office. "How soon can I come back and pick up everything?"

"As Doctor Redding may have explained, we begin by drilling for bone powder, then soaking in a buffer, followed by a silica extraction with centrifuge and other solutions just to obtain a small drop. The DNA is then located, copied and sequenced. Even with our advanced technology, it takes some time."

"Lucas told me six hours."

"The Doctor is accurate; however, circumstances can vary. If you would like to check back tomorrow, that will be fine."

The man seemed to know his stuff, and Joel could think of nothing else to ask. Through the glass partition, he observed the ordered layout of the central office. It all looked well organized with shelved items, scientific equipment, and award plaques on the walls. Other staff could now be seen circulating through a long hallway through connecting rooms.

Satisfied, Joel shook hands once again. "I will check back tomorrow."

"Can I assist you with anything else?" The voice came from a few feet behind.

Joel turned. It was a uniformed guard trying to force a smile. "No thank you. Just leaving."

Amber rode on the sailboat's blue canvas deck in her bathing suit, watching Joel as he pushed her into the breaking waves. After reaching the rolling swells, he locked down the twin rudders and pulled himself up beside her. She held the rudder arm as he tightened the billowing sail which started them moving quickly into deeper water.

"A perfect day for sailing," said Joel, "and I promise not to talk about mermaids."

"Thanks for calling. I needed this."

"It's relaxing and a fun way to get some sun. If you want to speed up, change course slightly to starboard."

"That's to the right?"

"You've got it."

"Wow, it really speeds up."

The fourteen-foot catamaran left a frothy trail beneath a clear blue sky as the wire halyards whistled and the port pontoon bumped up and down through the ocean swells.

"Tuck your feet in the loops," said Joel, sliding alongside her on the port side while further ratcheting in on the sail. Almost immediately their side lifted from the water.

"What do I do? We're tipping over."

"You're doing fine. Stay on course and we can hike out."

"Hike? Joel, we're on water."

"It means lean out, like this. Just hold on with your feet. Here we go." As he said it, up they went, and Amber let out a long shrill of excitement. A little more wind and it might have tipped, which sometimes happened and required lifting the wet sail and righting the boat, not part of the fun.

They continued hiking out and racing silently along, enjoying the view as the distant strip of beach sand grew narrower and the ocean beneath took on a darker hue. After a while Amber changed course into the wind sending the boom swinging suddenly in their direction.

Joel reached to shield Amber's head, but she had already ducked down. Receiving the rudder tiller from her, he brought the craft around while letting out the sail, then set a relaxing course back to land.

"Did I pass my sailing lesson?" said Amber, brushing her hair out of her eyes.

"Like a true First Mate."

"I almost hate to go back."

"I know the feeling."

"Joel, what did you do with the bone?"

"It's at a test lab."

"You let someone have it?"

"Just long enough to run a DNA analysis."

"Somehow I lost those pictures I took of the skeleton. Do you still have yours?"

"Sure. Right here," said Joel, patting his cell phone in his bathing suit pocket. "Waterproof."

"Are you going to take one of me sailing?"

"Hold it on course." Joel locked in the sail line and took out his camera-phone. "Are you going to pose?"

Amber hiked out holding the halyard with a big smile. "How's this?"

"Perfect." Joel snapped the photo, and another. Not bad, in any way. He made sure they were saved with a final check. Yes, those were saved, but those two were all the pictures he saw. *No others!*

"Is something wrong? You said it was perfect."

Joel was trying to scroll through his photo file, but everything had been erased. "They're gone."

"What's gone?"

"All my skeleton shots. I don't like the feel of this," said Joel. "How could the photos from both of our phones with all the skeleton shots be removed?"

Amber said it, even as Joel was thinking it, "Now all that's left is the bone." Even the newspaper photos lacked the detail needed for a scientific inquiry.

Joel's mind retraced all the people he knew that he had spoken to over the last few days, and how any of them could possibly be involved. Could anyone have influenced their service providers to take such an action? Nothing made any sense.

"When do you get the bone back?"

"Both Redding and the lab said it would take six hours. I was planning to pick it up in the morning."

"Dr. Lucas Redding? Isn't he the one who cut your interview short?"

"The same."

"And now he is suddenly interested in helping you?" Joel had a gnawing pain in the pit of his stomach, always a bad sign.

"I'll ride with you. Let's go get it today," Amber said.

Joel tightened the sail against the following wind and steered straight for the beach. They needed to change, gas up, and get a bite on the way, in time to be there before the lab closed.

It was close to 5:30 when Joel and Amber pulled into the Global-Tek lab parking lot and hastily made their way past the guard, through the lobby, and to the office window which was still open.

"We have an artifact and DNA analysis to pick up," said Joel, addressing a stern-looking woman wearing a lab coat.

"Name?"

"Joel Landon."

She neither looked down nor away. The silence felt strange.

"A DNA analysis was set up by Doctor Lucas Redding."

"What kind of item was it?"

"A jawbone."

"When was it brought in?"

"Between nine and nine-thirty this morning. I brought it in myself."

"Do you have a receipt?"

"No paperwork was needed."

"Who did you give it to?"

"A tall man in a business suit. He assured me that everything was pre-arranged and paid for."

"Sir, that may be the case, but no records with your name are in my file."

"You haven't even looked. What kind of operation do you run?"

"Mr. Landon, Global-Tek is a respected institution with the highest ratings. All our business is conducted with the highest standards. If you deposited something with us, the records should be here."

"Is your manager in?"

"We are currently in transition. The new management will not be in place for a week."

"I don't have a week to wait. I demand my bone with or without your analysis, immediately."

"Sir, I am very sorry for your mix-up, but we are closing for the day."

"There is no mix-up. You have my bone." As Joel was speaking, the woman was sliding the office window closed in his face. Irate, he rapped on it. The mirrored finish prevented him from seeing inside. Amber stood alongside him looking equally perplexed.

"You heard the lady. The office is closed. I must ask you to leave." The deep voice was from the guard standing behind them, his right hand poised above a black side-holster.

Joel and Amber expressed angry looks before submitting to the escort out of the building.

5

Lifting his eyes, Simon Johnson drew strength for the spiritual battle that he discerned was near. His own thoughts had to be taken captive. God's presence acknowledged. There was always some degree of warfare in and around the mobile chapel.

"You guys may not carry a tune in a bucket, but just the words will do us all some good." He glanced around the chapel at the seven truckers, six men and one woman, and at the open hymnal as they spoke together –

"I heard an old, old story, how a Savior came from glory, how He gave His life on Calvary to save a wretch like me; I heard about His groaning, of His precious blood's atoning, then I repented of my sins and won the victory."

"Anyone here done that?" Several heads nodded with eyes that joyfully glistened. After a pause, they continued with the chorus –

"O Victory in Jesus, my Savior forever, He sought me and bought me with His redeeming blood; He loved me ere I knew Him, and all my love is due Him, He plunged me to victory, beneath the cleansing flood."

"It sounds like a battle, Chaplain," said a driver.

"It is, but it's been won," said Simon.

"Then we don't have to fight?"

"You better believe there's a fight, just not the kind you can see."

"I handle things by myself," said another, with a dragon tattoo.

"If you know Jesus, you're not alone; but if you're not sure, you're in a very dangerous place," said Simon, exchanging glances. "Satan is real and has a strong gang. He's described in the Bible as the god of this world with the ability to deceive the nations. But Jesus is stronger."

"I've got a boy who's doing crack. Will you pray for him?" said the lady driver.

"I will. I want to pray for all of you and your families. And we can trust Almighty God to act."

Simon took time to share the good news of God's love and forgiveness through Jesus, then shared his testimony, which opened questions as to why Christians face such persecution in this present world. Two of the truckers, including the one with the dragon tattoo, saw their need of salvation and made the eternal exchange, their lives for new life in Jesus Christ.

In his closing prayer, Simon included the two earlier visitors, Joel and Amber, that God would protect them and help them to find the answers they were seeking.

"I'm not leaving this place without that bone," Joel fumed, staring across the street from the parking lot at the darkening Global-Tek lab building, "even if I have to wait here all night."

"Do you think that woman knew where the bone was?" asked Amber, pulling down the Jeep's visor- mirror on the passenger side.

"I've never been a conspiracy-theory kind of guy before, but I'll admit this has me wondering."

"Same here," said Amber, applying some fresh make-up in the dim light.

Judging from the few cars remaining, Joel figured that all the regular employees had gone home. Only the guard had come out in the last thirty minutes to walk around, smoke a cigarette, and go back inside. A night shift likely coming up. "I hope you don't mind waiting."

"Detective services don't come cheap." At least there was some humor remaining.

The sun was setting behind them, stretching shadows from the trees across the forest-green lawn of Global-Tek properties. Both Joel and Amber adjusted their car seats back a notch. Realistically, it wouldn't be long before they would need to visit the all-night McDonalds nearby, if they had to spend the night in the Jeep.

"Are we really doing this?" Amber's voice registered irritation.

"That bone isn't leaving that building until it's in my hands. I never should've left it."

"Okay, alright," she finally resolved. "I'm with you."

An hour had passed since the security lights had come on, and the guard completed another round.

There had been no traffic. Everything was quiet.

Then a car came into view. A black Mercedes. They watched as it rounded the corner and turned into the half-circle drive leading up to the main entrance.

"Unusual time for a visit," said Joel, raising his seat back to an upright position.

"What could they want?"

"We'll soon see." Joel was in full-alert mode. Anything was possible. He thought of getting out but didn't want any lights to signal their presence.

"It's a tall man," whispered Amber.

The driver who got out had the same stature as the one inside who had first taken the bone. Joel tried to process the surreal scene as a second man appeared in the doorway with a package—just the right size—handing it to the tall man who then opened the trunk and placed it inside. Closing the trunk, he then returned to the driver's seat and closed the car door as the second man disappeared back inside the building.

"This isn't happening," said Joel, cranking up his Jeep.

The Mercedes was already wheeling out of Global-Tek, into the street that joined a major highway. And Joel was following half a block behind.

"Are you going to stop him?"

"For now, I just need to keep him in sight."

Joel put the pedal to the floor once they got onto the main highway, turning on his headlights. The other car had leveled off at the speed limit, hopefully unaware that they had a tail. Joel decided to close the distance and get their tag number as soon as a semi moved out of the lane between them. With the opportunity, Joel sprang ahead, closing the gap.

But then, the Mercedes took off at an impossible rate of speed.

"I think we've been spotted," said Amber, trying to act calm.

Joel was silent, doing all he could to keep the other car's rear lights in sight. His speedometer climbed to 80–90–and higher while dangerously maneuvering in and out of traffic, horns of big rigs blasting. For a few minutes he was almost keeping contact, until the blue light special appeared in his rear-view mirror along with the twin bleeps of the patrol siren.

The chase was over.

Rather than talk about the bone, Joel just took the ticket.

"Where do we go from here?" said Amber.

Joel rested his head on the steering wheel. They hadn't moved from the side of the highway. There was no telling which road the black Mercedes might have taken after vanishing from sight. No bone. No clue.

"I think I got the tag number," she said.

There was hope. Joel lifted his head, took out his phone, and punched his father's number in Tallahassee. As a Senator he had the connections needed. After a few security questions, his father agreed to help with the basic information on the vehicle. Joel thought it best to avoid details of the lab test and resulting car chase, and the speeding ticket.

"It's registered to a private owner by the name of Donnelly, at 99 Lagoon Way, in your own community."

Joel swallowed silently. It was a familiar address.

"A gated development. Very wealthy folks," said his father. "Is there something more that you need to tell me?"

"Not at this time. Thanks."

Joel wasted no time in getting back on the road, and up to speed limit.

"How did I ever get into this?" said Amber, gazing through the window into the darkness.

"Your dog got lost in a hurricane."

No reply.

"And we found something we weren't supposed to see."

"A deformed sea cow," said Amber.

"Maybe. Maybe not."

"You're angry." Amber could sense it.

"Not at you."

"I hope not, but who?"

"99 Lagoon Way is the same location of Dr. Lucas Redding."

"The scientist you interviewed?"

"The same one I thought was doing me a favor by getting the bone tested."

"You're speeding."

Joel let up on the gas. Anger only partially described what he was feeling. Throw in betrayal and a heap of confusion. As he thought of past events, he continued to weave around traffic, through a long dark stretch, and finally onto the familiar Coastal Highway.

After about five more miles, Joel wheeled into the illuminated entrance of Lagoon Estates with its guard house and closed security gate.

They had to stop and wait as the heavy-weight official waddled out in full uniform, a shiny holster on his side, and clipboard in his left hand. Joel had already thrust an important-looking press card, compliments of Stu, through the Jeep window.

"Beaches News. We have an appointment."

"An appointment?" said the guard, giving a lift to his cap while eyeing the vehicle. "And where might this be?"

"Lagoon Way, 99."

"Ah…The Donnelly Estate."

"Can we go on?"

Officer spit-shine was taking his time with his pen and clipboard. "Just as soon as I complete the visitor check." He sauntered to the rear, noting the tag, then back into the guard house where he picked up a phone and made a call.

With phone still in hand, the guard leaned out the door. "They want to know who the appointment is with."

"Lucas Redding," said Joel, with no hesitation. His eyes were on the gate.

After a moment, the guard placed the phone down along with the board and re-emerged, looking less considerate. "Dr. Redding has no scheduled appointment this evening. I must ask you to back out and turn around." His right hand rested on his holster as he gestured with his left.

Mounting frustration simply took over as Joel popped the Jeep into drive and stomped the accelerator. Barely missing the gate arm, he plowed through a clump of palmettos and swerved back onto the drive, picking up speed.

Amber had been silently following the gate drama and was looking back. "Do you think he'll shoot?"

"Looked like an empty holster to me."

"Was that a smart thing to do?"

"We'll soon find out." Joel was already nearing the estate turn-off and anticipating a warning call from the guard. No telling how much time he had to find the evidence he needed.

"There's the Mercedes," said Amber, pointing to a carport at the rear of the driveway.

Joel abruptly stopped in front of the entrance as security lights came on. "You can stay in the car if you like."

"No way," said Amber, already getting out with Joel. "You may need a witness."

Joel pounded on the door as the progression of bell chimes sounded from within. They had to know he was there. Eventually, the dead bolt slowly turned, and the door opened a crack. The face of the butler appeared.

"State the nature of your business."

"It's urgent that I see Dr. Redding."

"Our guest is not expecting any visitors."

"Tell him Joel is here for his bone."

"I'm sure he has no idea what you're talking about."

"I have a crow-bar, and unless he wants that Mercedes trunk damaged, he better speak with me."

"Sir, I assure you we have nothing that belongs to—

"It's okay, Stephens. I'll see the young man." It was Lucas's deep voice from the hallway. The butler backed away allowing Redding to open the door.

"Joel, it's a little late for an interview."

"You know why I'm here."

"Should I?"

"The car out back has my bone from the lab. They wouldn't return it to me. We saw it put in the trunk and followed it here."

"You must be mistaken."

"There's one way to find out," said Joel. "Let's look in it now."

Redding turned and spoke, "Stephens, get the keys."

"Sir, there's a call from the gate-keeper. It seems that some damage was done by our unauthorized guests."

"It's okay, Stephens. I'll take care of it. Let's go satisfy our visitors now."

Joel and Amber silently followed Stephens and Redding around the side to the carport where the Mercedes was parked.

"You're positive that this is the car?" said Redding.

"That's the tag number," affirmed Amber. "Then let's have a look. Unlock it."

Stephens triggered the remote and the black trunk lifted. Joel and Amber stepped forward to see inside.

It was clean.

"What did you do with it?" Joel demanded. "Is it inside?"

"I never had it, my friend. You took it there for testing, and you were to pick it up."

"Somehow, they lost our records, and your man picked it up. We saw it all."

"I understand your frustration over the mix-up, but we would never do such a thing."

"Then, tell me. What was this car doing there, loading a two-foot package into this same trunk?" There was no question, the tag and vehicle description matched.

"Joel, you should not jump to false conclusions. An extraction kit had just arrived from China," said Lucas.

"We were picking it up for one of my clients which just happened to coincide with your visit."

Joel was at a loss for words, trading glances with Amber.

"Allow me to call the lab personally, first thing in the morning, to straighten this out."

Still silence.

"Go on home, you and your friend, and get some rest. Call me around noon tomorrow."

Having returned to his guest room at the Donnelly estate, Lucas sat down and reached into a drawer for his secure phone. He didn't trust the government, nor any of the world's governments, but he did take advantage of their encryption technology in his calls. The number he entered was in Washington, D.C.

"Lucas?"

"Who else did you expect?"

"How is the clean-up going?"

"Just a few details left."

"The lab report?"

"As expected, DNA sequences are a match with the skeleton."

"Excellent. Get it to Andros Base Lab."

"What about the Smithsonian?"

"Too risky. Can you handle the Senator's son without an incident?

"He'll buy into the story tomorrow."

"Very well. See that he does."

Connection closed.

6

The fiery sun continued its eastern climb as Joel jogged back to his seaside boat house, winding down from his run. The usual relaxation was shrouded by anxieties from the day before– the Global-Tek distrust, the suspicious package pursuit, and final confrontation with none other than Dr. Lucas Redding, renowned genetic scientist and elite advisor to DARPA. What more would have to happen in order to recover the missing fossil and get to the bottom of its origin?

Joel entered the bulkhead side door into the galley-office area, added some turtle food to Murf's box, and plopped down in his desk chair. His thoughts went first to Amber, how supportive she had been, and how well she had held up through the ordeal, which wasn't over.

"Rest up," he had told her when he dropped her off at Oceanside RV Park the night before.

"After a day on a roller coaster," Amber replied, "that will be easy."

At least some resolve was now in sight. One DNA test lab was about to get a shake-up. Joel visualized it with satisfaction, following the investigative call of Dr. Redding. Some inept handler, maybe two or three, would lose their jobs. It served them right for losing his bone. Best of all, maybe they'd be forced to find it.

Shortly after eleven, Joel called the number Lucas had provided.

"Ah, Joel. Good morning."

"Good morning, Doctor Redding. You said to call."

"It's Lucas, please. Let me be your friend."

That was the last thing Joel could imagine. "Have you had time to uncover the problem at the lab?"

Lucas's silence was unsettling.

"You've located my bone?"

"Joel, a most unfortunate event has taken place involving not just your specimen, but several others."

"What are you saying?"

"Joel, please hear me out. Following the drilling for the bone powder used in the DNA testing, the technician is directed by the tag to either return the specimen to the shelf, or to dispose of it. Do you recall any tag instructions given when you turned the specimen over to the lab?"

"No. Nothing was said about tag instructions."

"That appears to be the problem. There was a new processing technician at work the day you went in. She has been replaced."

"So, what happened?"

"The bone was officially discarded."

"You're saying my bone was thrown in the garbage? Where's the garbage?"

"Unfortunately, my friend, due to the high government standards imposed on laboratories, discarded specimens cannot be simply tossed out. Everything must be incinerated, daily."

Joel was quiet, swallowing hard. *Not good.*

"The good news, Joel, is that we have been able to locate the DNA analysis."

"Really?"

"Absolutely"

"What did it turn up?"

"In terms you would understand, one-hundred percent sea cow – just an anomaly. I'll have a copy sent to you."

Silence.

"Well, you certainly didn't expect a mermaid."

"I'm not sure."

"Come on, Joel. You're an educated person. That's the stuff of mythology."

The call was ended with two sharp raps on the door. "What else could happen?" he mumbled, as he got up, went to the door, and cautiously pulled it open.

"It's your partner in crime," said Amber, with a cute smile and wind-tossed hair. Her black lab, Midnight, was with her on a leash.

"Come on in," he said as she glanced in question at Midnight. "Sure, dogs are welcome; but better yet, let's enjoy the view. I'll meet you both topside on the aft deck. Coffee?"

"You must be a mind-reader."

In a few minutes Joel had dumb-waitered the coffee and two breakfast buns up from the galley, then sat down to join her at the round table. Midnight rested by a bowl of water Joel had included, leash hooked over a side cleat.

"How are you doing, and what's the news on the bone?" asked Amber after a first sip.

Joel looked up at the gently swaying tree limbs, and out at the waves. "Not so good."

"You've talked with the Doctor what's-his-name?"

"Right before you knocked."

"And he said?"

"It's been incinerated."

"How could that happen?"

"Something about tag instructions."

"There's nothing left?"

"Not a clue."

Amber gazed silently at the beach.

"Just the analysis."

Amber turned her face toward Joel, quizzically.

"The DNA analysis from the lab. Lucas, that is Doctor Redding, was able to retrieve it."

"Don't keep me in suspense."

"The test turned up nothing unusual. Just a sea cow, like we figured. Maybe a very old variety."

"That's what your doctor friend said." Amber's voice sounded skeptical.

"An anomaly." It was man's way of explaining the unexplainable.

Amber broke off a piece of her bun and dropped it in front of Midnight. "Do you have a problem with that?"

"You mean like the adventure being over? Case closed?"

"Well, yes." She was watching her dog lick the bun sugar from the wood-planked deck.

Joel had the vision of himself in a courtroom as a witness on trial. Was he comfortable with the evidence?

His thoughts then shifted to the scene on the beach several nights earlier. "It all just doesn't fit."

Amber looked up in silence.

"No one goes to that much trouble to remove a sea cow from the beach."

"Could it have been a dream? Sometimes our minds can play tricks on us."

"What I saw was real."

"But, the jawbone analysis–

"Thank you, Amber!" Suddenly, the missing photos, the lab report, the empty trunk, the phone conversation with Lucas–everything became a huge collapsing tower, far too many coincidences to be true.

"What did I do?"

"You helped me to question the evidence."

"What are you thinking?"

"If what I'm thinking is right, that doctor is definitely not my friend."

"He faked the analysis?"

"We could be facing the father of lies."

Joel slid the 12-foot aluminum Jon-boat down the bank into the south end of Green Port's lagoon. The sun was setting, and it would be dark enough by the time he arrived.

The small outboard engine cranked on the third pull and ran smoothly and reasonably quiet. Snaking northward through the darkening waterway, past banks of scrub palmettos and under bridges, the sole occupant reviewed his plan.

It was not the usual fishing and pleasure trip, but one born out of a sense of justice. It was not the customary time of day to be on the lagoon, but the intent was not to be expected.

There were gators that had their hidden dens along the way; but generally, they were no threat to the residents, only their pets. In the daytime their heads could be spotted on the surface. At nighttime the only way to see them was to catch the reflection of their glowing red eyes from a flashlight or full moon, unlike tonight.

Living on the Florida lagoon was a thing of status, like living on a coastal marsh was in Georgia. Selling multi-million-dollar homes to people, built on a swamp, was a Realtor's gift, one that he didn't have. Castle-like houses testified to the war of wealth and prestige. The game of golf was a great part of lagoon life with courses and cart bridges crossing the water and challenging its players. More than a few balls, even clubs, had been dragged from the muddy bottom by kids and caddies looking to make a few bucks.

A past incident came to mind, the memory of when a teenage boy was walking in the shallows, feeling for golf balls with his feet. An eleven-foot gator came from nowhere, seized him from underwater and began to pull him down. A nearby buddy heard his cry for help, came running, grabbed his arm and helped to pull him free. A single row of bite marks on his leg revealed that the gator had been missing a set of teeth, the only reason it hadn't held onto its prey.

Joel ducked as the boat passed under the last wooden bridge. He was familiar with the area.

Recognizing the docks, he throttled back. Silence was wise. The estate was not far away.

Deciding to do this was his idea. Amber didn't know and he didn't want to involve her or risk her safety. These people, if they were operating on the level he suspected, were playing for keeps. His mission was to make a way of entrance and to recover his bone, then to expose the cover-up of the century. He might even be promoted as Stu's partner or be offered a slick magazine writer's job.

As the Donnelly dock emerged through the darkness, Joel cut the motor and used his oars to row in silently. There were no dock lights, so he continued all the way to the platform and secured a line to a cleat. He had dressed in dark clothing and had a bag of tools he might need.

Nearing the house on foot, Joel stayed low and moved through the shadows. Seeing some rear windows illuminated, he decided they would be the ones he would go to first. Blinds that were fully deflected offered no visibility. Removing a small listening device from his bag, he suction-cupped it to the glass, then withdrew to some trees where he connected the ear- piece and listened.

Joel had read spy novels, but he soon realized that what he needed most was patience while waiting for any recognizable sounds to discern what was going on inside. The weather was warm and mosquito repellant was one thing he had forgotten. Near the lagoon mosquitoes were thick and had found a willing sacrifice, one who dared not slap.

After fifteen painful minutes with no noises, he moved to the next more-central window. It was a larger room. After transferring the listening device, he pressed his face to the base of the glass where the blind was barely parted. He could see through.

The bugs were still biting as Joel strained to make out the shapes in the room, while listening for voices. He had bought the cheap device at an electronics shop, being advertised as real spy gear – great for capturing evidence of an unfaithful spouse. If it worked well enough, he thought he could use it. Now he wished he had invested more with the staticky sounds in his ears.

With no way to tell what anyone was saying, Joel pressed his face tighter to the glass. There was the back of a man sitting at a table with the profile of Dr. Redding. A man was seated across the table that he did not recognize. After some minutes of garbled conversation, there was a discernable door knock, followed by the words, "Come in."

Joel let out a gasp as he watched the hall door open and the tall man enter, with the package in his arms– the same shape and size that he remembered leaving the lab in the Mercedes.

Just then, as he was leaning hard with his face against the window, an ear-splitting shriek like the siren of Alcatraz caused Joel's heart to jump. Spotlights flooded the grounds where he stood. Nowhere else to go, he fled back to the trees. Hearing the barking and seeing the shadows of running dogs, he leaped and grabbed a limb, swinging his legs out of reach barely as two snarling mouths passed under him.

The command to return to their cages came just as his grip was about to give. Then another man's voice that he recognized, "Joel, you can come down."

He let down his legs and dropped, speechless.

A military-type rifle was trained on him by a man in a suit, while another attached cuffs and locked them in place behind his back.

Lucas stepped closer looking around, then nodded to the guards to be dismissed.

"Why, Joel? What did you hope to accomplish sneaking around in the night? I thought we were friends."

Joel had no reply.

"What is it you wanted to see?"

From somewhere, a righteous boldness arose. "You know very well what it is."

"You tell me."

"It's the fossil you lied about; the tall man was holding in the room."

"That's what you want to see?" Lucas pulled out his phone and made a quick call.

Within a minute, the same tall man walked from the corner of the house with package in arms.

"Show it to our reporter," said Lucas. "Unwrap it and show it to him."

Joel watched with a mixture of fear and expectation as the tall man slowly pulled back the paper wrapping. There it was, predictably not his bone.

"Joel, you are looking at an instrument used for the extraction of DNA."

The sound of a police siren was winding down in the Donnelly driveway.

"It's unfortunate, Joel, but we must charge you with criminal trespass and invasion of privacy. Do you have any good reason before you go, to explain your behavior to all of us?"

"You bet I do." No longer able to keep it to himself, Joel expounded on how he personally witnessed the helicopters and beach invasion and the amphibious seizure of the strange skeleton on the beach where he lived."

Lucas listened without reply, then turned and nodded to the uniformed officers who escorted Joel away to their patrol car.

"This is a call from-'Joel Landon'. If you agree to accept this call, press 5 now…"

After some delay, Amber slowly touched the "5" on her keypad.

"Amber. Hey. It's me."

"What's going on? I'm in bed."

"Sorry. I'm in jail."

"What?"

"I'll explain later. Can you come and get me?"

"Where?"

"The police station. Downtown."

"Sure, as soon as I wake up, get dressed and have some breakfast."

"You're kidding. Right?"

"Of course. Just give me a few minutes."

Twenty minutes later, a blue VW bug angled into a space alongside a black Dodge Charger with GREEN PORT POLICE on the side. The driver stepped out and made a straight path through the double-glass doors and up to the counter. A tired officer looked up from his paper strewn desk on the other side.

"I'm here to pick up Joel Landon. Can we please make this quick?"

After raising his eyebrows and slowly setting down his mug, he pressed an intercom button and spoke, "You can bring out Landon. His ride is here."

For another five minutes Amber stood fidgeting and leaning on the marble counter while the officer continued reading and drinking his coffee. The rear door finally opened, and Joel appeared with a sheepish look and plastic belongings bag in hand. After signing a few papers, he was released on bond. Neither of them said a word until they were in the car.

Amber spoke first, "Is there something about you, other than the alcoholism that I need to know?"

"It's not what you may be thinking. I got caught at Redding's."

"You went back?"

"By boat. Last night."

"Are you CIA?"

"No, but I do know a few spy secrets."

"And you got caught."

"As you can see."

"Did you learn anything new?"

"The package we chased was lab equipment."

"And now you're a felon?"

"Trespassing is a misdemeanor."

"Good thing your dad is a Senator."

"It took some explaining, but he got me released."

Amber detoured through a Mickey D's drive- through, paid for a couple breakfast sandwiches with coffee, then continued south to Joel's. She got a glance of herself in the rearview mirror and didn't like what she saw. "We have to stop meeting like this."

"Agreed," said Joel, as he took a bite. "Do you have plans today?"

"Back to work."

"I was wondering about that."

"Dr. Lane's still a little upset I think."

"You didn't do anything wrong, did you?"

"He referred to it as unauthorized entrance to his private office."

"Sounds like trespassing."

"It wasn't at night."

"No, but it was a shade sneaky."

"Not as sneaky as yours, Mr. Spy." Amber spotted the drive, slowed, and exited the Coastal Highway.

"What are you doing after work?"

"No lagoon boat trips."

"Not a chance. It's impounded. I was thinking about dropping in on our chaplain friend, with some questions.

Amber pulled up to the boat house alongside Joel's Jeep. "Sure. Around six?"

"I'll pick you up then," said Joel, getting out and closing the door. He mouthed a "thank you" through the car window as she backed out, then he went inside.

"So, tell me little fellow, what's going on in this world." Joel tapped on the container of turtle food watching Murf as he lumbered over a few inches, stretched his neck and ate.

The phone interrupted him with an electronic bugle call, suitable for Stu, his editor-boss.

"Writer's cramp," he answered. "Good morning."

"Hardly. Heard you had quite a night."

"You mean—"

"Exactly. Your run-in with the law. What were you trying to do?"

"It was a big mistake."

"I'll say, and it wasn't the first."

"I had reason to think that Dr. Redding was concealing evidence."

"So, you invaded their property by stealth after crashing their security gate earlier?"

"It was a mistake, Stu."

"More than a mistake, Joel."

Silence.

"Two businesses have said they're pulling their ads because you work for me. Ted Donnelly has phoned the county commissioners to beef up lagoon security, which will raise all of our taxes."

Silence.

"Do you have any idea who you're dealing with?"

"I'm beginning to see."

"I don't think you do."

Joel sat down, still holding the phone to his ear in silence.

"Joel, forget the article on lagoon life. Go find a seashell and come up with something profound."

"Click–" The call was over.

Joel felt like Murf looked–a beat-down turtle, just trudging along. It wasn't a day for any thoughtful work. He unlatched the hull door behind him and walked out to the beach.

The waves were monotonous, the gull cries annoying, and the sand like endless labor. What sense did it all make? What value was there to life? There were times he thought that he had answers, but then they were dismissed by doubts. How fragile and transient it all seemed. No wonder people drank and did drugs, to forget it all. Good thing he didn't have a bottle handy. Soon Joel had walked to the spot that was embedded in his memory. The giant dune was in front of him that once held the fossil skeleton. He kicked at the base of the slope. Just a sea cow. Lab analysis says a sea cow.

Anyway, at six he would see Amber. And they would pay another visit to the Oasis Truck Stop and Good News Chapel. Any answers would be a help at this point, he thought, glad that he still had Simon's number.

Few college graduates wind up working in the field of their major. Dreams change with education. That fact couldn't have been truer for Simon Johnson, who not only majored in vertebrate biology, but taught it while in graduate school. Now he was a chaplain to truck drivers, able to share the Biblical origin of life, and the Creator's love for man, more fulfilled than ever. Having a degree meant nothing to him compared to having a moment-by-moment relationship with the risen Lord Jesus Christ.

"How about some good news for a change?" Simon spoke, holding out a flyer to one of the drivers returning from the fuel desk.

The trucker paused and reached out. "Thanks, I could use some of that." It was a reply he heard often in a lonely line of work that daily tested a man's patience. Sometimes the reply was, "There's no such thing as good news," to which Simon would elicit conversation in hopes of relieving a burden. He was a good listener and had gained the trust of the truck-stop management, a helpful guy to have around, and good for business.

Around 6:30 PM he was on his way back to the chapel trailer, having gotten a call earlier that Joel and Amber wanted to meet with him. They were waiting at the front steps. "Hope I didn't keep you two waiting."

"Just got here," said Joel.

"Come on in. It's usually open."

Inside, they settled into some chairs facing each other.

"Can I offer you some bottled water? I can make some coffee."

"We're fine, thank you," said Amber.

"Well, the last time, as I remember, we got into an unusual subject. How can I help you this time?"

"Actually, it's concerning the same subject as before," said Joel.

"Which is maybe crazy to even be talking about," added Amber.

"We need to know if such a thing is even possible," said Joel.

"A mermaid?" asked Simon.

"Or something like one," said Joel.

"You first need to know that the Bible is my authority, not human opinion. Are you okay with that?"

"We need answers," said Joel.

"I could give you a lesson on vertebrate biology based on evolutionary teaching, but it's in conflict with God's word. And that won't give you any answer."

"Go on, please," said Amber.

"For understanding we need to go back to the beginning."

"Well, I was walking my dog on the beach in the storm—"

"Not that beginning, but the beginning of mankind." Having their attention, Simon went on, "Life as we see it today does not offer much of a clue to the beauty and blessings of earth's early days following what God calls a very good creation.

"We live on a battleground, a planet that was once ripped apart by a worldwide flood – a judgment of God upon part of His own creation that rebelled against His holy ways, both angels and men. Another final judgment is still ahead.

"Adam was a special creation apart from the animals, made in the image and likeness of God. This infuriated those angels who were proud of their position. They violated God's order by taking human women as wives which produced giant offspring, the heroes of old.

"They continued their evil and through terrible acts corrupted all flesh, as documented in Genesis, Chapter Six."

"Even the fish?"

"All flesh. Fish have a flesh of their own, just as birds and land animals differ."

"Why would the angels do that?"

"A good question, and for that answer we must go back to the garden, in Genesis 3:15. The judgment that God pronounced on Satan for causing man to sin would be executed through a coming Seed that is Jesus. The fallen angels under Lucifer, or Satan, were aware of this prophecy and determined to do everything they could to prevent it, including massive human slaughters and corruption—even to the genetic alteration of humanity, merging one form of creation with another."

"Do you want to know what we found?" asked Joel.

"Can you show me?"

"That's the problem." Joel went on to recap the main events and a detailed description of the skeleton.

Simon listened with interest. The way in which it had been removed from the beach was the strongest evidence to Simon. "If all you found was a Manatee, someone has made a costly mistake. But if what you found is trans-human, testifying to the truth of God's word, then you may be in the middle of a high-level war. But with God's Son on your side and His Spirit inside, don't be afraid. Just make sure He is."

7

"Pecan encrusted Mahi-Mahi. It's one of our chef's favorites," said Ted Donnelly, seated at one end of the formal dining table.

"Very nice," responded Lucas Redding from the other end.

Four other guests were also being attended by two white-coated servants who passed back and forth through a swinging door to the kitchen.

Lucas was giving little thought to the food, or the service, or the accommodations at the Donnelly estate, as he lifted a fork of bean and almond casserole from the gold-rimmed plate, then set it back down.

"Do you think we will be bothered again by the young reporter?" said Ted.

"No," answered Lucas. There was more he could have said; but neither Ted nor his guests were in the loop to hear of any plans beyond what concerned his estate, which Ted would not have owned were it not for Lucas's network.

"We're state-of-the-art equipped to handle intruders. The dogs can be quite a strong deterrent."

"They were quick," injected one of the guests who had been present the night before.

"That reminds me," said Ted, glancing at one of his servants, "both dogs are due for a treatment. Can you take them first thing in the morning?"

"Yes, sir. No problem."

Lucas lifted a chunk of fish and put it in his mouth. As he bit down, he felt a sharp needle-like pain. Reflexively, he leaned over and cough- ejected a mouthful back onto his plate. Still hurting, he felt with his finger around his teeth, searching for the source of his discomfort. At last he found it and extracted the pointed bone.

All had turned their attention to Dr. Redding. "Are you alright, Doctor?" said the host, moving his hand below the table edge and pressing the call buzzer.

The sound soon brought the entire staff to the room. Lucas was dabbing at his mouth with the white linen napkin which displayed a spot of red.

"It's the fish," said Lucas. "Doesn't your chef take out the bones?"

"We're very sorry, sir. The fillet is not supposed to have any," said a server.

"Well it does," said Donnelly, defending his distinguished guest.

"Can we get you another piece, sir?" asked the other server.

"I've had enough." Lucas pushed himself away from the table.

"Throw the rest away," said Ted, as Lucas got up to leave. "Can we get you anything?"

"I'll be fine," said Lucas on his way out.

"Will you still be joining us for the festival luncheon tomorrow at the Surf Club? We are looking forward to having you as our honored guest and speaker."

"That is still in my plans." It was an important day for the locals—their Green Port Festival. All the staff would be gone, given the day off.

His mouth still sore, Lucas retired to his guest quarters. There he saw a blinking light, the signal that he needed to respond to a call on his secure phone.

"Lucas here."

"And how is the doctor proceeding with his patient?" Lucas was irritated by the veiled way in which the powers sometimes spoke, but understood the need for secrecy, even with scrambling technology. Hackers, given the time and money, could find a way in. And information was power.

"The doctor," said Lucas, "is delaying his departure." "The patient didn't agree with the diagnosis?" "There have been some challenges."

"Elaborate."

"Arrangements are being made for surgery."

"I assume the doctor will exercise caution, given the delicate condition of this patient. Friends and family may object."

"You can be assured that our arrangements will leave no room for objections."

"Lucas, this is why you are in the position you are. We have full confidence that you will do whatever is necessary."

"Don't worry. It will be a clean procedure and will all be over in a few days."

"Then back to the lab?"

"As planned."

Lucas closed the line, took a deep breath, and rested his head against the cushioned back of his chair. Terrible tasting fish.

Distant trumpets and drums signaled a band prepping for the parade. Joel followed the morning smell of coffee through the main street entrance to Starbucks. He had about twenty minutes to grab some wake-up and find a front patio seat before everything started. Fortunately, the line was fast. He did not expect any delays. But the unexpected happened as the counter clerk apparently recognized him.

"Joel Landon? It's Joel Landon, everybody!"

Joel looked around awkwardly as other Starbucks' employees and customers spotted him.

"You're our man, Joel," came a shout.

"Look, guys," the clerk said, pointing to a clipping on the wall. "It's the reporter who discovered our mermaid, right here on the beach in Green Port."

Joel looked closer. It was the article Stu had put together with the heading, "Manatee Mermaid Gives Visitors a Thrill," with two photos showing Joel along with the grainy skeleton, which someone had colored. "I had no idea what it was," said Joel, trying to be truthful.

"Well, we know what it was, don't we?" shouted the clerk.

"Mermaid! Mermaid! Mermaid!" The chanting arose and kept going strong, until the clerk who started it lifted her hands and clapped, which began a wild applause.

When the encore finally settled down, the clerk spoke again, "Joel, your coffee is on us. Starbucks' mermaid wants you to have it for finding her." Joel had noticed the artsy mermaid logo before but hadn't thought that much about it.

"How did you keep from being lured to your death?" a customer asked.

Another clerk said, "You can interview Shannon here. She saw one early this morning, sitting on a piling under our pier."

Joel smiled, thanked the establishment, and took his free coffee outside to a seat.

It was the perfect day for a parade. Not a cloud. In the mid-seventies. People lined the downtown street trying to keep their young ones close, away from the approaching start-up float, a giant pink crab with a banner – "Welcome to Green Port Annual Claw Festival."

He would have enjoyed Amber's company, but she had to work. Joel needed to work too but wasn't too inspired over writing an article on a seashell, assuming Stu was serious.

He watched as a column of shiny convertibles rolled by carrying waving girls and local dignitaries. Then came the rumble and roar of the Harleys as their local chapter showed off their bikes. After a brief gap, the brass and percussion of a marching band was heard as blue and white uniforms preceded by twirling majorettes made their turn onto the main street.

Then a booming voice came over the loudspeaker saying, "Let's hear it for the Green Port High Marching Tritons."

Joel paused before taking another swallow of his coffee, as the word "Tritons" jogged his memory bank. Simon had used the word, even read the description of one from an early Greek physicians' account, then had shown Joel in the Bible where such a thing might have happened in ancient history. The connection with the band's name was somewhat unsettling.

After the band passed, there was another gap of space, then a deep, prolonged blast from a long horn, and a huge balloon float appeared. When the drone of the horn ended, the booming voice from the parade speakers said, "Make way for King Neptune, triton of the sea."

Tritons—too many to be coincidental—had Joel's attention. Now he watched one bobbing against its restraining cords, the giant helium-filled representation of a merman, with a barnacled human torso and the tail of a fish. A stern countenance glared down beneath a tarnished crown, and a three-pointed spear (trident) protruded from its billowy right hand.

A hush of awe swept over the onlookers as some removed their hats. Most held back their children who were eager to rush out and touch the swaying figure. Then the left hand slowly rose with a large conch shell in its grasp. As it touched Neptune's bearded mouth, the horn sounded again, so loudly this time that the children retreated, clinging to their parents for protection.

Without finishing his coffee, Joel tossed it with its logo into the trash, got up and left.

Spraying water against the kennel's concrete floor wasn't Ambers favorite work, but she was glad to still have her job at Beaches Animal Clinic and liked being around most of the dogs. Only a few made her nervous, like the two large pits in pen six. They had been dropped off earlier for rabies vaccinations, Bordetella shots and fecal tests which had been completed by eleven.

After completing her morning tasks, she was asked by Dr. Lane to deliver the two black pits back to their owner.

"Dave, their keeper, usually picks them up, but he got the day off and a fishing trip planned. You can handle them. Just keep their muzzle guards on till they're inside the gate."

Amber reached out and took the two sets of keys to their van and the customer's dog gate.

"When you're done with the dogs, leave the gate key just inside the rear servant's entrance door to the main house. Dave said he would leave it open for you. Lock it as you leave."

Amber walked each of the pit bulls to the clinic van with a short leash, muzzle guards attached. No problem. She then started the engine and checked the address – 99 Lagoon Way. It seemed too familiar.

The drive didn't take long but became more difficult on her nerves the closer she got to the location. She passed through the same security station that Joel had damaged, drove down the same street, and arrived at the very same estate to which they had gone earlier, chasing the suspected fossil jawbone. It was the same place Joel had been arrested for his secret spy venture, which had failed to locate the fossil, if in fact it was there.

Turning into the Donnelly estate, the white van made its way around the driveway, passing the main entrance and continuing down the side until the private dog kennels came into view surrounded by high fencing and warning signs.

Amber parked and checked the kennel gate key. It opened. She then led each of the big dogs from the van to the gate. Safely removing their plastic muzzle guards, she released them inside the area and re-locked the gate. At first, they were busy running around and sniffing out their familiar domain. Then abruptly, they shifted into a defensive-aggressive mode, forgetting the hand that had brought them safely home, snarling and growling at the gate with fangs bared.

Thankful to leave them behind, Amber proceeded to the back side-door of the main house as instructed. There were no other vehicles parked on the property, no signs of activity or noise other than the low growls and fence clawing from the kennels.

Instructions had been to leave the kennel key inside the door, which she found unlocked, and to lock the door as she left. There was a side table inside that seemed the logical place to set the key, which she did.

Amber should have left immediately; but something inside compelled her to look around, to take a few steps and look a little further. If someone was there, she could say that she was just making sure that someone got the key.

As she ventured further into the main estate, it occurred to her that just possibly, somewhere here, she could find the bone. Up until now it had been Joel who took the risks to get it back. Now she had the opportunity to do something, even if it was just to satisfy their curiosity.

All was quiet. There were no sounds from inside that she could hear, no reason to worry that someone might surprise her. Still she walked softly. The thought that she might be the one to recover the stolen artifact heightened her senses as she explored here and there, in cabinets high and low, in one room then another.

Eventually she came to a hallway that led past several closet doors. At the end was a heavier, more ornate door, which when tried, opened.

Inside, the large room was subdivided with a comfortable seating area and wet bar, with a bedroom to the back. Someone obviously was staying here and working on something, judging from the papers and folders. Arrangement wasn't neat and tidy to impress visitors but like a business office with numerous active projects.

There were built-in bookcases with sliding panels to lower cabinets. Amber first checked the obvious, then the concealed for the tell-tale package. Nothing resembled it on the open shelves, and nothing was found by opening the panels.

Next she hastened to the bedroom and opened the closet door. Nothing but a few hanging clothes. A chest of drawers sat in the bedroom corner. Methodically she slid open the top drawer, lifted and viewed contents, then worked her way down. The bottom drawer was heavier to slide open. On the top were some towels. Beneath the towels her hand met paper. It was a bag.

Ambers heart pounded as she slowly lifted the package from the drawer, then opened it and looked inside.

Incredible as it seemed, there was the jawbone. Amber had found it.

On the way back to the animal clinic, she detoured by the Oceanside RV Park and stopped at her trailer. She carried the package inside, putting it in the hidden utility closet in the back room, then shut the door to keep Midnight away from it. It was the safest place she could think of at the time. She also decided to keep the discovery quiet, even from Joel for now. He was a newsman and might say something too soon. There were bad people involved and Amber just didn't want either of them to get hurt.

"My name is Joel and I'm a recovering alcoholic." It was his turn to speak in the meeting, and he was still wrestling with what to call himself. He didn't like thinking of himself as an alcoholic and wondered if words had any power. At least it seemed honest. There had been several times he came close to having a drink recently or at least had thought about it. He guessed that made him one.

Amber was absent. He wasn't sure why but quit speculating about it as the meeting progressed.

"I'll be reading from the AA book," said Father Robert, at least that's how most addressed him. He was a Catholic priest, the one who usually officiated over the sessions.

Joel flipped open the front cover of the used book he had been handed, noticing all the hash marks someone had made inside under a penned heading, "Days I have been here."

Robert began reading, "We alcoholics are men and women who have lost the ability to control our drinking. We know that no real alcoholic ever recovers control...We have seen the truth demonstrated again and again – once an alcoholic, always an alcoholic."

He paused and looked around the gathering. No eyes were looking up, but Joel's. Their eyes met. "Would you like to share with the group?"

Joel swallowed hard before replying. "That's pretty much the way it's been for me since dropping out of college. Sure, these meetings have helped, but I've been wondering lately why we don't read from the Bible.

"In our last meeting at Chaplain Johnson's, he pointed out some things– "

"Let me clarify that," interrupted the priest. "Alcoholics Anonymous represents those from all different faiths and strives to maintain an atmosphere of acceptance to everyone who comes for help. We would not force a Christian to read the Koran. Neither do we force a Muslim or Buddhist to read from the Christian Bible. Does that make sense?" Heads nodded around the room.

"I suppose so," said Joel.

"We encourage everyone to seek their own higher power, whoever or whatever that may be."

"But what if our only victory is found in Jesus?" Joel sensed a shockwave through the room as the Name left his mouth. All eyes were on Father Robert waiting for his reply.

Robert coughed and turned uncomfortably in his chair, then looked harshly at Joel. "Let's remember the rules."

The reading continued without any answer to his question, but Joel was barely listening. Scripture Simon had shown him kept going through his mind – *"Jesus said, I am the way…no man can come to the Father except by me,"* and *"If any man is in Christ, he is a new creation. Old things have passed away. All things have become new."* It was true. Those of other faiths would not feel at ease with the words of Jesus. But for Joel, there was a new-found hope.

When the evening meeting closed and the circle disbanded, Joel noticed a text on his phone from Amber – "Visiting a friend." That being the case, he decided to stop by and see Simon on his way home. The chapel was open late for anyone who wanted to talk.

A tractor-trailer from Covenant Transport was backing into a space as Joel pulled his Jeep around and into a place next to the chapel trailer. He got out and tapped on the door.

"It's open," came Simon's voice.

"Got time for a few more questions?" said Joel, stepping inside.

"Always. It's good to see you again, Joel."

"Better to be seen than viewed, as they say," said Joel, pulling up a seat.

"You've got that right. What's up?"

"Well, I just left the AA meeting."

"And."

"I sort of understand why they avoid the Bible, but I thought it was Christian."

"Well, years ago it was started by Christians, like many of our ivy league colleges. But over time, to gain broader acceptance, they suppressed the truth."

"So, what about all those other faiths?"

"Joel, everyone has faith in something. For many in this country, it's their money. It's the object of our faith that ultimately matters."

Silence.

"Which one has the power to change your life? Only one religious leader died for our sins and was raised from the dead."

"I don't see guys changed that much in the meetings."

"Most of them relapse or change addictions."

"Sadly, I know," said Simon, resting his hand on his Bible. "They don't understand the authority of this book."

"What makes it so different from all the other religious books?" Joel truly wanted to know.

"It's the One who authored it. Although men penned it, God breathed it in such a way that the words are from God Himself. They tell about His Son who was sent to earth to redeem mankind."

"What if I choose to ignore it? It seems kind of narrow."

"I tell truckers they are free to cross over to oncoming lanes of traffic. There is a broad way that leads to destruction. Biblical truth according to Jesus is narrow and few truly find it."

"I've heard there are many paths to God."

"Joel, your salvation was very costly to God the Father. If there had been any other way for mankind to escape eternal judgment, then the crucifixion of His Son was in vain. There is only one name under heaven given among men whereby we must be saved – Jesus."

"This discussion is getting kind of deep, and it's late. Maybe we can talk more about this another day."

"I'll be waiting. Just don't wait too long. Let's pray before you leave."

8

An hour, maybe two had passed since Joel had stopped by the chapel for a visit. Simon had dozed off with the Bible in his lap open to Psalm 91, the passage on Divine protection.

His eyes snapped open at the sound of metallic tapping. It wasn't at the door of the trailer, like a driver seeking entrance, and it was too late for most visitors.

The tapping came again, this time louder, from somewhere on the side. Simon pushed himself up from his chair and went to the door. No pole lights had been installed, though promised by management, so it was dark as he stepped outside except for the faint yellow light near the door.

The noise had stopped. At the foot of the steps he paused, waiting for his eyes to adjust to the barely visible surroundings.

"Hey chaplain," said a man from the shadows. "We want to talk."

Simon had a check in his spirit but continued to advance in the direction of the voice. "How can I help you?"

"Actually, it's more like how we can help you."

"Help me?"

Gradually, three human forms became distinguishable, one on each side and one ahead, all wearing dark clothing and ski masks.

"We want to keep you from getting seriously hurt," said the man in front.

Simon caught the reflections from the hands of the two men on the sides—brass knuckles.

"Do you have any fear of death, man of God?"

For some unnatural reason Simon was calm. His faith hadn't been tested in this way before, but he had no doubt in the power of His God and the promises of His Word. "Why should I fear those who only have the power to kill the body?" he replied. "The One to fear is He who has the power to cast both body and soul into hell. Are the three of you ready to face Him?"

"Shut up, chaplain," said the leader. "I could shoot you right now, but that's not why we're here." The two on the sides were getting closer.

"What do you want?"

"Stop meeting with that newspaper reporter."

"Joel?"

"That's the one. He was here earlier with his wild stories, the mermaid man."

"I don't control who comes to visit the chapel."

"Well, man of God, when we get finished with you, you will control who you talk with. It would be a shame to see such a nice little chapel go up in flames, along with the chaplain."

As the men on each side moved in, preparing to swing, Simon spoke one word. It was the Name that.had been given all authority in heaven and earth—

"JESUS."

Whether He chose to deliver Simon or not, He was still his Lord, and His future kingdom would one day swallow up the darkness in righteous judgment. He had perfect peace.

As soon as the Name left his lips, three sets of semi headlights suddenly bathed the entire area in light along with a roar of diesel engines. The darkness was split apart with every man and every movement visible. Nothing hidden. The three attackers looked around to see who was watching.

"Good evening, Chaplain," came a deep strong voice from the lights. "Are these guys giving you a problem?"

Seven truckers emerged, bigger and taller than any he had ever seen, brandishing long pipes, stepping toward his three attackers.

The three looked frantic for a way of escape.

"I believe these fellows were ready to go home and do some praying," said Simon, looking hard at the masked leader. "Am I right?"

The one in the middle exercised some good sense and nodded.

"But before they do, they each need to take one of my booklets with them," Simon said as he reached into his shirt pocket and handed them each a copy with the heading, "Would You Like to Know God Personally?"

As soon as the three were out of sight, Simon looked around to thank the huge truckers, but they were gone. The engines had quieted, and the headlights were off. A great sense of awe and thankfulness welled up within him as he returned to the trailer.

Inside he sat down again in his chair and looked at his open Bible. There within Psalm 91, verses 9-11 leaped off the page as he read them:

"Because you have made the LORD, my refuge, the Most High, your dwelling place, no evil shall befall you, nor shall any plague come near your dwelling; for He shall give His angels charge over you, to keep you in all your ways."

Simon prayerfully considered the threat spoken concerning Joel. Time was so short and the need to make disciples so urgent.

"You summoned?" Dracor had made his entrance moments earlier into the estate guest room.

Lucas stood between the dark angel and the room with the chest-of-drawers, one of which was still half open. "I need information immediately."

"We know who has your fossil. What we have trouble learning is how you humans can be so stupid as to leave your doors open."

"How did it happen and who has it?"

"While all of you took the day off for the festival, an employee of the Beaches Animal Clinic returned some dogs and took advantage of an open door to do more than deposit the keys."

"That makes no sense," said Lucas, wondering why someone would go through the house and take only that package.

"It does when you know who the woman is. You should be familiar with her by now."

"Who is this woman?"

"The same one who was here once before with the Senator's son – Joel's girl-friend, Amber Wells."

They got it back. Lucas was pacing and his mind racing, growing infuriated. "Where is the package? I assume your spirits have followed it all."

"We have eyes in places you would never guess. Animals as well as humans make adequate hosts, even bugs will do. The bone is in her trailer, but so far she is keeping quiet about it."

"Is she a candidate for the base lab?" Lucas was forming a plan.

"She's given ground. We can get more."

"Then do it. I want her."

Dracor was rubbing his scaly head against the ceiling when the secure line rang.

"Doctor Redding," came the familiar voice
"Speaking."

"We understand that the doctor is missing his package and the surgical room has not yet been cleaned." Code talk.

"Clean-up is requiring special arrangements but will soon be done."

"Let me make this as clear as possible. Our pride in our doctor's proficiency has suffered a serious blow which may affect his future usefulness. Be smart and don't lose the package again."

"I assure you that not only will we have the package delivered, but a boost to our lab work as well.

"We will soon see." The call was over.

"It seems that you humans have your hands full," said Dracor as he unfurled his leathery black wings.

"You could have let me know sooner."

"You didn't ask." With that, Dracor flapped his wings and was gone.

Lucas poured himself a full glass of scotch. It was midnight and his right hand was trembling.

A train of dark clouds lined the morning horizon, breaking in one spot enough to send a sparkling path over the rippling waters. With the surf spilling over his feet, Joel stood at the ocean's edge, his mind not so much on the panorama as the location. It was the very spot where he had witnessed the amphibious vehicle disappear with the skeleton.

It had been no dream, he was certain. Maybe better if it had been. All the misunderstandings and trouble they had been through would never have happened. But now, sea cow or not, life would go on.

Joel extracted one foot from the sand suction of the outgoing tide and took a few crunch steps through a trail of coquina shells, myriads of tiny clam-like beings that had released their temporary hold on life. He looked at them in their pastel assortments of sunlit color and considered their human usefulness, past and present, in walls of forts and architectural design.

Maybe Stu would like such an article, tracing the lifecycle, beauty and building qualities of Green Port's coquina. The more he mulled it over, the less he thought of it as a redemptive work. More was needed to restore his reputation as a local news writer.

Joel returned to his boat house. Coffee was made and morning chores needed doing early in preparation for Amber's birthday. He had a few surprises planned.

After getting the place ship-shape, Joel got into his Jeep and drove downtown. He pulled into a family bakery with the name, Sweet Expressions, that was known for its award-winning cheesecakes. There he selected a crème brulee with an apple glaze. His next visit was a few doors down at the Beaches Gift Shop.

Amber worked till three. It was shortly after five when Joel picked her up. As planned, they went to see a movie, a light and entertaining feature, titled E.T. Returns. Reviews had been mixed and choices slim at the Beachview Theatre.

"How do they come up with little creatures like that?" asked Joel afterward.

"I want to take one back," said Amber. "They're cute."

"Midnight might object."

"Then I might just have to *go home* with it."

"Let's have some pizza first."

"Sounds like fun." Amber flipped her hair as Joel made a hard turn into the drive-through at the Pizza Palace.

Soon they were headed back to Joel's where they would eat and celebrate her birthday. A little time remained before sunset which allowed them to enjoy the view from the upper deck, seated at the round table. Everything was in place upon arrival.

Amber re-sectioned the pizza slices while Joel brought up some non-alcoholic drinks and a small gift-wrapped package.

"For me?" Amber wore her usual attractive smile, a loose light-blue shirt, white shorts and sandals. There was some mystery in her eyes.

"You're the birthday girl."

"Should I open it now?"

"As soon as you like." Joel poured the bubbly grape drink as Amber unwrapped and opened the box.

Her lips parted and eyes shone with delight as she lifted the silver chain necklace for a closer look at what was attached. "It's a baby sand dollar. How perfect."

"Payment for entering my beach."

"Your beach. How could I forget?" There was moisture in Amber's eyes as she lifted her auburn hair and connected the necklace. "I could not have imagined a better birthday gift."

"Even getting our fossil back?"

Amber's eyes suddenly closed and reopened with a far-a-way look.

"Sorry. Guess I shouldn't have brought that up," said Joel.

"It's alright. Let's enjoy the pizza."

"And we've got some of your favorite cheese-cake for later."

"Crème brulee?"

"From Sweet Expressions." Joel was hoping to see the relaxed happiness return to her face, but something was bothering her.

Neither of them said much as they bit into their pizza and sipped on their drinks. The early evening breeze ruffled their napkins while a distant gull sounded a series of cries.

"Joel." Amber broke the silence in an unusual business-like way, "I have a surprise for you as well."

His mind went blank.

"Remember the day of the festival when I had to work?"

"Yes. I missed you.

"There were some dogs I had to return to an estate on Lagoon Drive."

"Not *that* estate."

"The very same one. Donnelly's."

"Go on."

"While returning the keys I was able to get inside."

Joel put down his pizza and sat back with a dumbfounded expression.

"Joel—I found it!"

"The jawbone?"

"In the bottom drawer of a guest-room dresser."

Joel was speechless. *Lucas was a liar. The whole thing had been a lie.*

"I got it back for you."

"Did anyone see you?"

"No one was home."

"Are you sure?"

"Completely. All the cars were gone."

"What did you do with it?"

"It's hidden in my trailer. I was afraid if I brought it to you that you would get yourself in more trouble."

Joel considered what he might in fact do with it now, armed with this added information.

"If you want it back, you can have it; but I don't mind keeping it until you decide."

The proverbial ball (bone in this case) was back in his court.

9

Joel had kissed her that night on her birthday, after taking Amber home. She wondered how he felt about their relationship. He seemed happy. She wasn't sure but wanted him to be. Fumbling through her keys, Amber finally found the small silver door key, twisted it and went in.

Midnight was immediately at her feet, whining more than usual for the expected belly rub, followed by a treat.

"It's okay, boy. I won't be going out tonight. Just you and me." Midnight seemed satisfied and calmed down with more attention.

The night before she had attended a graduation party at a friend's house, although it turned into more than that when one of the guests showed up with a Ouija board. Thinking why not, Amber played along placing her fingers as instructed on the planchette. To her surprise it started moving under some mysterious force, stopping over letters to spell words in answer to their questions. Nothing impressed her much until she asked about her future. The game piece without hesitation moved to the letters T-R-I-P. A shiver ran up her arm. It was so weird.

After putting a chewy snack down for the dog and freshening his water, Amber turned on the TV, picked up the remote and tried to relax while punching through the channels but was unable to find anything of interest. The movies were replays. She picked up a book she had started a week earlier, read a couple of chapters, then decided to go on to bed.

She unhooked the sand-dollar necklace, looked at it again more closely, and placed it on her bedside table. She then exchanged her clothes for a comfortable cotton sleeping shirt. After plumping her down pillow and turning off the lamp, she tried to relax and go to sleep.

About thirty minutes passed. Midnight wasn't sleeping either, his nail's clicking on the tile floor as he traversed the passageway between the front and back rooms. Amber got up following the night-light to the bathroom medicine cabinet, reached inside and found the Lunesta bottle. She tapped one of the blue pills into her hand and swallowed it with some water, then returned to bed.

It wasn't long before the pharmaceutical sleep-aid took hold and Amber was able to relax, drifting deeper and deeper into another dimension—a dream-world of soothing rest, where time and expectations no longer mattered. Peaceful scenes of white sand beaches and sailing with Joel over translucent aqua seas were as real as if she were there. She could touch the water as rainbow fish swam by and happy dogs leaped playfully through the shallows of the surf. Everything was so perfect, she never wanted to leave.

But then the wind began to whistle through the rigging of their boat, and clouds grew gray and stormy as the sea churned and tossed them about. Amber's heart raced and her hands clutched the sail sheets for stability.

Suddenly the scene shifted to the giant face of a Ouija board. She watched in nervous silence as the game piece slid by itself over the letters, re-spelling the same word that had been etched in her memory bank from the night before—TRIP.

Music began to play, sounding like Scottish bagpipes. It was an old song by The Beatles, "Lucy in the Sky with Diamonds." Abstract swatches of color replaced earlier images. Another tune started, "White Rabbit," by Jefferson

Airplane, as the colors changed like a kaleidoscope. Then it all stopped.

Her eyes popped open. Everything was silent and dark. Amber knew that something was about to happen. Like the feeling one got when the roller coaster slowly climbed to its apex. The time had come and there was no getting off.

A square in the ceiling above her bed began to glow, faintly at first, then more, as a beam of light entered the room. Midnight growled from just outside her bedroom door. She was frightened, yet at the same time curious. The light did not impress her as dangerous, but she had never seen or heard of anything like it. She thought of screaming or calling 911, but instead decided to wait.

Her bed was now bathed in a bluish light. Amber lay still staring upward. She was not conscious of any other presence besides Midnight, until something moved. Amber turned her head. Standing in the doorway was a short grayish figure about four feet in height with huge dark almond-shaped eyes and a small slit of a mouth, like E.T. in the movie she had seen.

Conditioned by the Hollywood creation, Amber put away her fears. She knew how the scene would play out. As the cute little fellow awkwardly advanced, she anticipated an out-of-this-world experience that few people ever dreamed of really happening.

This was far better than welcoming a new animal at the clinic. This was a higher form of life from some distant planet. How was it possible that she could be so privileged?

Barely two feet from her pillow, E.T. extended that long index finder, just like in the film. Her response was automatic. Reaching out she touched the tip of the finger with her own. Immediately she felt a bonding of their spirits. She was glued, fascinated with its features.

Then the little mouth opened, and the child-like words came out, "Come home. Take a trip with me."

Amber nodded before realizing that the beam of blue light had intensified like a giant glove around her. But then she relaxed, submitting fully to the force that she felt was in control. She had experienced vivid dreams in the past and knew what it was like to have a sensational dream. But this was far more, involving every fiber of her being, with senses fully alert and cognizant.

She was not on a boat, but she was lifting, slowly upward toward the ceiling. As she got closer, the ceiling appeared less solid as if de-materializing. She looked around for her friendly guide. The little guy had disappeared and reappeared with a package under his arm, like the one she had hidden in the utility closet. She thought of saying something but was too enraptured by all that was taking place.

Together the two of them drifted higher and higher, somehow passing through the trailer roof, lifted by the mysterious power of the blue beam. Beyond and above the trailer, and the surrounding trees, hovered a large circular object with lights around its perimeter. It made no sound as its transport beam drew up and received the incoming occupants.

Inside the silvery craft, Amber was moved by the same invisible hand to a metal table which reminded her of the one in the clinic where they operated on animals. She was growing less comfortable in this new location and unsettled by the appearance of the other occupants that seemed to be in charge. They were not little and cute, but large and reptilian, with a mean streak.

As straps were secured to Amber's arms and legs, pinning her in position, she felt something she had not anticipated–a wave of fear. The movie was over. *"Please let this be a dream. Let me wake up."*

Stu's got to jump on this. This story will launch Beaches News into the national spotlight. Joel was already envisioning his expose of government and scientific corruption and cover-up as he swung open the door to The Beaches News, bee-lining straight to his boss in the back. The wall clock pointed to ten.

His entrance was not missed by Sal, the editor's main helper. "Good morning, Joel."

"A very good morning it is," he replied, without breaking stride.

As usual, Stuart Glover was buried in papers with a phone to his ear. "Yes, we got the wire. Are you sure of the facts? No local witnesses? Of course, it was early. Thanks— Hi Joel. Pull up a chair."

Joel waited a few seconds to get Stu's full attention, though that was never a guarantee. He waited too long—

"Did you do the shell article?"

"Strap into your seat, Stu. You've been wanting big-time attention. I've got it for you. No one will call The Beaches News a mullet wrapper after this."

"Must be some shell," said Stu with half-raised eye-lids.

"No shell. Remember the fossil jawbone?"

"The lost one that got you arrested?"

"It's no longer lost, Stu. And guess who had it?"

"You tell me."

"None other than the famous Dr. Lucas Redding."

"You're telling me that you found part of a sea-cow skeleton."

"There has to be more to it. Lucas lied about its disappearance, brought it home from the lab, and probably faked the report."

"How did you get it?"

"A very reliable friend recovered it from the Donnelly estate."

"Who is—?"

"Amber Wells. She works for Dr. Lane at the Animal Clinic."

"Amber Wells?"

"Yes, that's her name."

"Forget the story and go home. We don't want any connection with her." Stu pushed the piece of paper across his desk to Joel. "We just got it."

It was a government fax for "Immediate Release" which Joel picked up and read, "Green Port, Florida. Female, Amber Wells, Arrested 2 AM at a Trailer Home in Oceanside R.V. Park by Federal Narcotics Squad. Charged with Drug Theft from Beaches Animal Clinic. A 10cc Vial of Ketamine (Class III Drug) was found in her possession, a Federal Offense."

Stuart Glover picked up his pencil and resumed his work as Joel laid the note back down on his desk, slowly got up and walked out of The Beaches News office.

"That was quick," said Sal, as Joel passed without reply.

There was no answer as Joel repeatedly called Amber's phone on his way to the RV Park. His mind was in disbelief. It made no sense. *Drug theft? Amber?* The ten-minute drive seemed like eternity. Joel wheeled the Jeep down the narrow entranceway over a speed bump, past the wood-framed office, to the trailers at the rear.

As he pulled up and parked, Joel was a little surprised to see her unit not roped off with yellow crime-scene tape after the description given in the government fax. It looked the same as before with the potted flower by the front door. Maybe the whole thing was a mistake. He knocked, then pushed against the door. It opened.

"Hello. Anyone home?"

Inside, there was the smell of dog poop. Light from the windows was enough to see around. Joel went first to the living and kitchen area. Nothing seemed out of place, but some cabinet doors were open. He then walked into Amber's bedroom. The covers were in a pile at the foot of the bed. The clothes Joel remembered her last wearing were on a hook just inside her closet. He then felt a lump in his throat as his eyes focused on the sand-dollar necklace on the bedside table.

A surge of guilt swept over Joel for Amber's safety, as he thought about letting her keep the recovered fossil in her trailer, especially after all the trouble surrounding it. He wondered if it might still be there as he continued to explore the spaces more carefully.

The door to a small utility closet in the back room of the trailer was wide open. To Joel it seemed like a good hiding place for the bone, but there was nothing there except a sweeper and some cleaning supplies. Could they have taken the bone while searching for drugs? And where was the dog?

"Is someone here?" came a man's voice.

"Yes, here in the back," said Joel, "a friend of Amber."

The two men met in the hallway, then moved outside. It was the property manager wearing a paint-spattered T-shirt with a suspicious look on his face.

"I'm Joel Landon, just stopped by to check on her."

"Guess ya haven't heard."

"Heard what?" Sometimes more was learned by playing ignorant.

"Taken away on drug charges. We try to keep a clean rep around here and this happens."

"Any idea where she was taken?"

"Aint you the dude with the local paper?"

"I write a little."

"The mermaid guy who lives in the boat just up the beach?"

"That's me. Did you happen to see any of this?"

"Nope. Sound asleep. I don't move around like some do at two and three in the mornin'."

"How did you find out?"

"Got a call a little while ago."

"local police?"

"The feds. That girl got herself in serious doo-doo."

"Did they take the dog? Black lab."

"Didn't say. Wife said she heard some barkin'."

"What happens to her place?"

"Nuthin' for now. Rent's paid for another month. Then we'll see."

Joel took out a pen and notepad from his pocket, scribbling and tearing off a sheet. "Here's my number. Please give me a call if you learn anything else about this."

"Hey, you won't play this up in your paper, will you? I can't afford to lose any campers."

"I'll do what I can, but I'm not the editor."

"Stu Glover. Does he still run the local mullet wrapper?"

"He's the one. Owner and editor." "I just may give ol' Stu a call."

"Sorry, I didn't get your name."

"I didn't give it. Ed. Just say you spoke to Ed."

"Okay, Ed. Gotta run."

"Got a fresh pot o' coffee on, if ya wanta sit 'n jaw fer a spell."

"Thanks. Maybe later, Ed."

Joel hopped into his Jeep and headed straight home. He had calls to make.

Murf was scratching around in his box, a sign he was hungry. Joel was too. After a short feeding break, telephone work resumed, with the difficult goal of discovering where Amber had been taken.

Calls were made to local, county, and federal law enforcement agencies, Sheriff's office, Florida Bureau of Investigation, Federal Bureau of Investigation, Bureau of Alcohol, Tobacco, Firearms & Explosives, even to Crime, Trauma, Death Scene & Bio-Terrorism Clean-up—every related phone number that Joel could find.

No one could help. Nothing was on record in their respective agencies regarding a drug arrest the night before at Oceanside RV Park.

Joel's frustration level was beginning to conjure up thoughts of having a real drink when the ship's bell clanged outside the hull door. He wasn't ready for an interruption but decided to take an afternoon break and see who it was.

"Finding your home is an adventure."

"Simon Johnson." Completely unexpected.

"If this isn't a good time, I can– "

"It's good. Actually, a great time. Come on in."

"I'm kind of messy from helping a driver. Can we sit outside?"

"Dirt's no problem, but the deck view is nice. Go on up. Steps are in the back. I'll meet you there. Iced tea?"

"Much appreciated."

Shortly, Joel brought out a couple glasses and sat down at the round table with Simon. "This is a change. The Chaplain visits me."

"I hope you know, Joel, it's more than a job. You and Amber have been in my prayers."

Joel gave a nod of appreciation, wondering how prayer worked, and how long it took.

Simon stretched and took a drink while scanning the surrounding seascape. The place was new to him. "So, what's changed?"

"Do you want the short form or a long one?"

"I'm here to help. Take your time."

Joel was ready to open up, and felt that he could trust Simon. For the next hour, pausing only to respond to questions and tip his glass, he covered all the details beginning with the initial discovery, his interview and later encounters with Dr. Lucas Redding, the pre-dawn skeleton snatching by an amphibious team, and growing unbelief of his boss. Then he continued into Amber's own experiences at the animal clinic, their trip to the lab, the fossil pursuit with Joel's arrest, and finally Amber's account of the fossil recovery followed by her reported arrest for drug theft. "That's about it."

"Joel, how well do you know Amber?"

"There's nothing serious, like sexual, between us; but we've been close friends for a while.

"Did she use drugs?"

"I don't think so."

"Just checking."

"You're not suggesting– "

"Not really. I'd like to believe the best."

Silence.

"One thing I know. You're in a battle."

"That's for sure. I can't even find where they took her."

"The battle isn't so much with people, Joel. Our real enemy is invisible." Simon took a small Bible from his shirt pocket, opened it to Ephesians 6, and read –

"We wrestle not against flesh and blood, but against principalities, against powers, against the rulers of the darkness of this world, against spiritual wickedness in high places."

Simon closed the book. "It helps to know who and where our true enemy is. We don't fight what we can see. The enemy would like for us to think that, to keep us from praying and trusting in the One who has the power to bring us victory. Without spiritual understanding, men are mere pawns in the battle for men's souls. Some men learn through the mistakes they make, me included. We advance faster by reading the right Book."

"I need to be doing that."

"Without the Author's help, it won't make much sense."

"What do you mean? The ones who wrote the Bible are dead."

"I'm referring to the God who breathed out His Word by divine inspiration through the writers. And no, they're all still very much alive, just not here."

"So, how do I get His help?"

"Very simple. Seek it."

"And what happens when doctor devil gets in my face?"

"Pull out your badge."

"Get real." Joel pushed his empty glass to the center of the table.

"Even the devils operate under authority. If you're a believer in Jesus Christ, you wear a badge of blood with the highest possible authority, and they know it. But you need to know it too."

Silence.

"Joel, I sense in my spirit that you're more than a storm chaser. You've been beat by the turbulence long enough. Now you're being called to go into the storm. It's the only way you'll go through it."

"Will you pray for me?"

"Let me first ask you, Joel, have you ever been born again?" Simon was having difficulty connecting with Joel's gaze.

"I'm really not into religion."

"I'm not talking about religion, my friend. It's relationship."

Joel scooted his chair back. "Do you mind if we continue this a little later?"

Simon stood up with him. "I hope we can," he said, smiling and shaking hands, "but don't be surprised if the storm gets in the way."

The two walked down and around to the side, where Joel thanked Simon for his visit and Simon promised to pray for him, then handed him his pocket Bible. A gift.

10

The weather the following morning wasn't kind. Rain stung Joel's face as he pressed through a two-mile beach run. He found it therapeutic, helping to take his mind off recent setbacks, though concern for Amber was a heaviness that could not be run off. Lightning flashed with the crackle of thunder close behind as he decided to cut it short and head back.

Feeling better after a shower, Joel picked up the pocket Bible he had left on his desk, flipped it open and glanced at a few words. It seemed distant, like something written for someone else. Maybe he needed some help in understanding it, but for now closed it and slipped it into his pants pocket for imagined protection.

The phrase "into the storm" was rolling through his mind. Simon had used it in a predictive way that Joel couldn't seem to shake. He wasn't sure what it meant, but the more he meditated on it, the clearer it became; and at the center of the storm was one man–Lucas Redding.

With some help from phone information, Joel got the number for Ted Donnelly on Lagoon Drive. His plan was simple and direct. He would confront the respected Doctor with the facts and see how he handled them. The call went through.

"This is the Donnelly estate. May I help you?"

"Yes, you may," said Joel. "I need to speak to Doctor Lucas Redding."

"Doctor Redding has departed."

"How soon will he be back?"

"The Doctor will not be returning anytime soon."

"He's gone from Green Port?"

"Most definitely."

"Do you know where he was going?"

"Our guests do not divulge their plans with the help."

"Did he leave a number where someone might reach him?"

"I am sorry, but I am unable to provide any personal information on our guests. You might try reaching him through one of his offices."

"Is there one you might suggest?"

"You can try the Smithsonian in Washington."

Joel thanked him and went through a network of extensions.

"Out of the country on business," was all he got.

Turning to his computer, he googled "U.S. Department of Justice". If Amber was in federal custody, there had to be some way to locate her. Finally, after a series of selections, he found the "Federal Inmate Locator", and typed in "Amber Wells, White, 27, Female", and hit "Search".

"Results – 0"

Suddenly, with an electric pop, the power went out. The monitor screen went dark along with the lights in the house.

Joel sat silent, tapping his fingers on the desk, then picked up his phone placing a call to his father in Tallahassee.

"You have reached the office of Senator Landon. Please press 1 for English. Press 2 for Spanish. Or press 3 for– "

Joel jabbed the number needed while mumbling about voice mail, and at last got a ring.

Another robotic voice, "If you wish your senator to approve article 361, press 1. To disapprove, press 2. To leave a message for your senator, press 3. To reach the operator, press 4."

Joel jabbed 4 and took a deep breath as the connection changed and the line rang four times–

"Hello, Senator Landon's office. Katina speaking."

"Katina, put me through to Senator Landon. It's important."

"I'm sorry, but the Senator is away on business today. Would you like to leave a message?"

"This is Joel Landon, his son. I need to speak with him."

"Joel? Oh, hi. Wish I could help, but he's gone for the day."

"Did he leave a number where he can be reached?"

"I'm sorry, Joel. He didn't, but he will be back in the office tomorrow."

Joel closed the call, clenched his fists, got up and paced back and forth. "Relax. Everything will work out. Amber will turn up, and the truth will finally be known. Isn't that right Murf?"

His turtle had withdrawn his head.

"You're not speaking either. Bet some food will draw you out." Joel tapped some pellets into the box.

Just then the lights returned and the computer rebooted, as his phone rang, displaying the main number and ID of The Beaches News.

"Hello, Stu?"

"This is Helen, the new receptionist. Is this Joel?"

"In the flesh."

"Joel, Mr. Glover wants you to come in at 3 PM today for a very important meeting. It's about the bone fossil."

"Have they found it?"

"I don't know, but it is essential that you be here sharply at three."

"I'll be there."

"That's what I'm talking about Murf. Things are already turning around. Ol' Stu is finally getting hold of the truth. Everything's gonna work out. Amber's going to turn up. Gotta think positive, Murf. Just think positive." Joel did a dance while Murf continued eating.

Five till three, Joel got out of his Jeep, straightened his shirt and entered The Beaches News building. Helen was at her new receptionist desk, looking the part.

"Good afternoon, Mr. Landon. Mr. Glover and the others are ready for you in the conference room."

"And I've been ready for this," said Joel, heading for the wide wooden door on the left. Stu had obviously grasped the importance of such a discovery to have pulled such a meeting together.

Joel was ready for bear as he swung open the door but was disarmed by the identities of those gathered around the table. As soon as he stepped into the room, two white-suited men stepped from behind and stood on both sides of him.

"Please be seated, Joel," said Stu.

Confusion swept over him as he was guided to the chair, noting unfriendly countenances all around, including his own father's. What was he doing here?

"Our county attorney, Tom Faircloth, will explain the legal reasons why you are here," said Stu, nodding to the man across from him.

"Joel," Tom began, pausing as if pondering the state of the galaxy. As an educated citizen you are certainly aware of the laws of privacy that govern our nation."

"I don't know what you mean. What is all this about?"

"Ed Barnes, next to me, is ready to testify under oath that yesterday you unlawfully entered one of his units at Oceanside RV Park. Would you like to comment on that?"

"The door was unlocked and a friend of mine lived there."

"Was your friend there?"

"No."

"The fact is Joel, you were aware that your friend, Amber Wells, had already been arrested by federal agents on serious drug theft charges. Your employer, Mr. Glover, had let you read the government fax."

"That's true, but I was looking for something that belonged to me."

"Mr. Barnes said that you removed nothing from the trailer."

"That's right. I couldn't find it."

"You should have checked first with the park manager. What was it you were hoping to find?"

"A fossil."

"Was it the mermaid fossil, Joel?"

"Yes. We were hoping to get it DNA tested again."

"Joel, in front of each of us is a copy of the lab test that was performed on the subject bone by a respected DNA testing facility in Orlando. As you can see, the results show that your fossil is from nothing more than a sea-cow."

"It's a fake report, meant to hide the truth." There was a collective sigh through the gathering.

"Why did you think Ms. Wells had the bone in her possession?"

"She recovered it from Dr. Lucas Redding's room at the Donnelly estate."

"Did anyone see her with it?"

"No. She was returning some dogs and went inside to drop off the gate keys. While there she looked around and found it in a guest room."

"If this is true, both of you could be charged. Fortunately, we have the owner of the estate, Mr. Donnelly, with us. Ted, would you care to comment?"

"Yes, Tom. I know about the dogs being returned, but there was no way any person could have entered the house without setting off security alarms and cameras. To accuse our well-known guest of having a stolen artifact, even from a sea-cow, is very offensive and a defamation of character."

"Ted, where did you find the gate keys?"

"Beneath the mat at the back entrance."

"Thank you, Ted. We apologize for any wrongful insinuation in this matter. You may be excused." Donnelly left the room as the attorney continued, "This takes us to the main reason for our meeting. We want to thank Senator Landon for coming, Sheriff Blake, Father Roberts who oversees a local chapter of Alcoholics Anonymous, and Doctor Lamb, a psychiatrist with Global-Tek Institutional and Humanitarian Services and his assistants.

"As a lawyer, I have spent considerable time on the phone and with many discussing this issue. I assure you, Joel, that all of us want only to do what's in the best interest for you and society.

"There is a threshold of behavior that once crossed, instigates the need for intervention. There are those who deeply care about their family member, friend and employee, and felt obligated to sign the necessary legal forms. Everything is in order, Joel, for you to receive the kind of restorative care needed."

"What intervention? You can't do this. I'm getting out of here," said Joel, pushing his chair back.

Two firm hands came down on his shoulders.

"This is an involuntary judicial emergency commitment," said Faircloth.

"It is all in your best interest, son," said Father Roberts.

"Just relax," said Dr. Lamb, as he suddenly plunged a needle into Joel's upper arm which was being gripped securely by his assistant.

In moments Joel entered La-La Land. As he was shuffled to a white van, he recognized the blurred lettering, *Global-Tek*, but nothing mattered anymore.

Lucas Redding watched the familiar landmarks, bridges and architecture of Rome shrink in size as the seven thousand pounds of thrust from the twin Allied Signal turbofan engines lifted the silver Learjet, Starling, through the clouds on its transatlantic return from the Vatican. Enroute to Andros Island, the two passengers were comfortably buckled into their plush leather seats across from each other, under a satisfying two-zone temperature control and 72-decibel noise level suppression.

The Starling leveled off at a cruising speed of 437 knots and the seat belts were released. With the push of a service button, an attractive uniformed stewardess appeared.

"Would the Doctor and his guest like a drink?"

"Is it too early?" asked the Jesuit priest with a wide smile.

"Not at all," replied Lucas. "Whatever and whenever you like."

"I believe I will have a bloody Mary."

"And you, sir?"

"Bring me my usual. Scotch."

While their orders were being filled, Lucas rotated his seat to better converse. Father Magruder did the same.

"This is the way to travel," said his guest.

"Indeed. The Starling was a nice gift from the government which I have found quite expedient, and comfortable." Lucas lifted the leg rest. "The lever is on the side."

His guest found the lever. "Should I call you father?"

"Heavens no. Please, just Malcolm. Or, if you prefer, Mac." He looked relaxed in a casual polo shirt under a cardigan sweater.

"I thought you people wore black shirts with the little white-collar thing."

"A plastic tab. Never liked it. Kind of irritates the neck. Aren't you scientists supposed to be wearing white lab coats?"

Lucas chuckled without comment.

"Actually, Jesuits have quite a variety of clothing. We dress to fit, and wear the collar when saying Mass. What we wear is usually determined by the diocese in which we're working."

"You call it work?"

"I should give you a tour, when we have time," said Mac, returning the grin.

"Time to explore the archives of the Vatican. Hopefully we can." Lucas had gotten a glimpse of it once under high-level security and knew that it held secrets.

Both men paused as the stewardess silently set their drinks in the collapsible trays next to them.

"Isn't it providential that the two of us would be flying together—a Jason scientist and a Jesuit priest, chief representatives of the two primary pillars which undergird and control our world system?" said Magruder, thoughtfully looking up.

"Did you ever believe in the so-called God of the Bible?" Lucas felt at ease in posing the question.

"An interesting, but outdated book. Certainly worthy of study but not intellectually satisfying," Mac replied. "And you?"

"Never saw the need for such a One. All the questions we have can be answered rationally and scientifically in light of evolution."

"No gray areas?" Mac took a sip of his tangy tomato juice and opened a bag of nuts.

Lucas thought before responding. "Until recently, the origin of life, with its biological order and complexity, presented a challenge; but now we know."

Their eyes met with mutual agreement.

"Deep down, I always knew it was them," said Lucas, lifting his glass.

11

Global-Tek's conglomerate of operations occupied three buildings and thirty acres with testing laboratory, institutional treatment facility and administrative offices, arranged in a triangle around the parking area. Joel had been too sedated to recognize any of it at the time of his arrival. Since then he had learned of his location from remarks by one of the orderlies who brought food rations to him twice a day. He had also gotten a glimpse of the testing lab through his window when the blinds were adjusted by a medications nurse. They were left closed.

"Do you know how much shame and grief you have caused your family, the embarrassment you have brought on your employer, the confusion you have created within your community, all because of a misperception?" Relentless questions and accusations hammered at him nightly by an interrogator beneath a bright light kept him from going to sleep.

"Why are you doing this to me? I only know what I saw." Joel's replies fell on deaf ears.

"Do you understand how your perceptions can be affected by your beliefs? Are you aware that your own father is a founding supporter of Global-Tek? We hold to the highest ethical standards in all our laboratory reporting."

Joel knew some of the tactics of mind control–sensory deprivation, imbalance of diet, reflective interrogation to produce guilt–he had seen it in a movie, but he was poorly prepared to play it out on the receiving end. This first week had been the breaking-down phase and, combined with the unknown medication, was working.

Despite his inner resolve to stay strong and hold fast to what he knew to be true, he was weakening under the examining doctor's barrage of reasons to change his mind about everything he had experienced. It was now the skeletal anomaly, the soldiers of the sea hallucination, and Amber's drug-induced claims. Everything could be explained away. The bones could have been carried away by scavenging birds or animals. Dreams can sometimes seem like reality. People can radically change when using drugs. It all seemed to make sense.

Then came the promise of relief from the tight restraints, a move to a more comfortable and spacious room with freedom to move around, watch television, and enjoy three delicious meals a day with snacks and drinks of his choice.

"Surely you can see how such thinking was a danger to society," said the interrogator, "and required our intervention."

"I suppose."

"Do you want to be transferred from the restrictive unit?"

"That would be nice."

"Good, Joel. We want it too." The doctor opened his folder laying a paper and pen on the rolling tray before him.

"What's this?"

"Just a simple form for you to sign that you agree with us and give consent to further treatment."

With his arm ties loosened, Joel held the paper closer, but the words were blurry. He remembered a warning his father ingrained to not sign anything without knowing what it means. "What does it say?"

"It's basically saying that you agree with Global-Tek's diagnosis of your condition, as we have discussed, and are ready to make the changes necessary for reintegration into society."

"Admitting I was wrong?"

"Yes, Joel."

"About everything I believed?"

"Just sign at the bottom. We're ready to move you out of here." An orderly was entering the room with a wheelchair.

"No way."

"What?"

"No way will I sign that."

Joel saw the smile turn to a scowl on the doctor's face. He retracted the pen and paper, sent back the orderly after reattaching the restraints, and then left the room in darkness and silence.

"Am I crazy?' said Joel to the walls.

The following week was a repeat of the first, with a different examiner in charge who took the task of mind control to a different level. Food was tasteless mush, morning medication was by injection, there was full-body restraint, lower light, and an odor that permeated the room like rancid cheese. A new technique of interrogation was used.

"Joel, tonight is a new night. I want you to take a deep breath and let it out as you gaze into the spinning, spiraling wheel in front of you." The voice was like that of a trusted grandfather reading a bed-time story. "Are you fully relaxed?"

"I could be if you people would leave me alone." Joel had played with a hypno-wheel borrowed from the psychology class in his college dorm years earlier, so the procedure was not unfamiliar. But instead of prepping students for an exam, or for a laugh with a post-hypnotic suggestion, this was to serve a shadier purpose.

"Listen to my voice, Joel, as you watch the wheel. I am your friend."

"Friend?" Joel was unable to see the man behind him who was speaking.

"Cast all your worries into the deep, deep well. See them disappear one-by-one as they all go down. Now just relax."

"As I count down from three to one, you will go into a deep, peaceful sleep. Let the wheel draw you down, down, down, into that deeply relaxing sleep. Do exactly as I say as I now count, three–two–one. Can you still hear me?"

"Yes."

"Great. Now while you are sleeping, Joel, I want you to go back to the night you first heard the helicopters over your beach. You got up and went outside. Do you see them?"

"Yes."

"Look down the beach. Do you see the boat with wheels and the men around it?"

"Yes, they are loading a long box."

"Okay, Joel. Now I want you to go back inside to your bed and lie down. Are you there?"

"Yes."

"Everything you just saw was a dream–the helicopters, the amphibious vehicle, the box–it all was just a dream. Now, I'm going to count from one to three and you will wake up. You will remember nothing that I have said. All that you will remember is that everything you saw was a dream, just a dream. And you will gladly sign the paper. Do you understand?"

"Yes."

"One–two–three. Wake up!"

Joel blinked and looked around as the wheel stopped turning. The tray on wheels was positioned in front of him with the paper and pen.

"The pen is there for you," said the doctor, watching as Joel slowly reached with his loosened right hand to pick up the pen. "Now sign."

Joel seized the pen and threw it down. "No way!" He watched as the hypnotist jerked up his wheel and walked out shaking his head.

Simon awoke sensing a presence. It was a peaceful presence, not that of evil which he had learned to discern through experience. He looked at his bedside clock. It showed 5 AM. He folded back the covers, got up and put on his clothes.

He followed an inner leading through the trailer, then outside.

Simon stood on the wooden deck, surveying the double row of tractor-trailers with their shaded sleeper cabs. The salt air from the nearby ocean was mixed with the scent of diesel fuel. Too early to walk the lot. What was it that had drawn him? As he waited and watched, he detected movement to his right, then heard music–

It was a driver in his cab and the peaceful sound of praise singing coming through his open window. The man had parked his rig alongside the chapel and was having a time of worship, something Simon rarely observed.

"Is that you, chaplain?"

Simon waved and walked over to meet him. "Good morning. Sounds like you're getting off to a good start."

The driver turned the music down and stepped out of the cab. His side lights were turned on so the two could see each other. "It's the way I like to start every day. Without Him I'm lost."

"You need to share that with more truckers, especially the young ones coming on."

"You've got that right." He was a short man in his forties with a salt and pepper beard, extending his hand. "Name's Gabby."

"Glad to meet you, Gabby. I'm Simon and I get the privilege of meeting you guys."

"And praying for us."

"Would you like to sit down in the chapel? I can put on some coffee."

"I would but got a tight schedule. Actually, the reason I'm here may be hard to believe."

"Try me."

Gabby lifted his eyes and his face shined as he looked intently at Simon. "Our Lord and Maker, Jesus Christ, wants you to know that He approves of your work and commends you for the way in which you sacrifice yourself in service to others.

"You have had challenges and faced them well by faith. Now a great task is ahead of you to give help to one of the Lord's choosing–his name is Joel.

"Receive God's strength and protection for the journey that will take you…" Gabby paused, shaking his head.

"Take me where? asked Simon."

Gabby's eyes were teared as he finished the sentence, "…to the gates of hell."

Simon stared at this driver named Gabby whose countenance glowed like an angel. If it was a message from God, it would happen. He had no doubt.

After giving Simon a hug, Gabby climbed back up into his International cab, gave a nod, then pulled out onto the highway.

Simon returned to the chapel and waited in prayer for daylight. Considering the words spoken, he had seen some hell-like activities, but never anything dark as "the gates of hell". He opened his Bible to Ephesians, Chapter Six, carefully reading about the spiritual armor required for those in God's army.

At first light, he found Joel's number, punched it into his phone and waited. With no response, he tried again later. And again, later, with still no answer.

Finally, Simon decided to drive to Joel's boat house. Upon arriving, he found the door open and the inside in disarray–drawers pulled out and cabinets open, papers and items scattered on both lower and upper levels alike. There was no sign of Joel. If it was vandalism he didn't know, but he engaged the lock as he closed the door and headed back to the chapel. Even the turtle was missing.

Doctor hypnosis had stormed out so befuddled that he failed to notice Joel's signing arm. With all the precautions taken, they had not re-strapped his right arm. Despite his grogginess, Joel managed to work the straps loose from his other arm, then his waist and legs. Then he pulled the drip needle with its adhesive from his skin.

His appeal to the administration for a case review hadn't worked, neither had he been granted permission to make a phone call. Global-Tek institution was looking more like Dr. Moreau's laboratory. Desperation called for desperate measures and Joel was determined to escape.

The room was small, twelve by twelve, built securely with block walls. Joel saw only two ways out, the door being the most obvious. Hall security cameras and guards could be a problem. He tried to twist the handle, but it wouldn't move, and he couldn't see or feel any lock release.

Joel walked to the window in the dim light and raised the blinds. Everything was dark except for some distant spots in the central parking lot. He tapped the tinted glass with a knuckle. It was solid and built in with nothing to raise. At least there were no bars, probably to keep from presenting a prison image to visitors on the outside. With the institutionalized doped up and strapped down, it was hard to imagine anyone getting out without Global-Tek's permission.

Pieces of furniture were few beside the bed—the rolling tray and a chair. The tray had potential, more than the chair, as it had metal corners extending beyond the rolling base, and he didn't feel strong enough to swing a chair. As Joel positioned the tray and considered the risk of being heard, a rumble came from outside—*thunder*. Just in time and getting closer. He waited until the flash of lightning, and then shoved the tray with all his might into the glass. There was a loud crack, but it didn't break. The thunder came too late, failing to mask the noise.

Joel heard voices from the hall and footsteps approaching. Quickly, he lowered the blind and scrambled back into the bed just as the door opened and a flashlight scanned the room. He held his breath, with drip tube and arms under the cover.

In a couple of minutes that seemed like eternity, Joel heard the remote call and voice of the guard, "All clear. Nothing to report." He listened to the clicks of the door-lock re-engaging and the footsteps of the guard returning to his station.

The storm had intensified. Lightning pops and booms of thunder were close, and rain was pelting the glass.

Joel slid out of bed and repositioned his battering ram. With a silent plea for help, he took a deep breath and lunged at the window, impacting the tray's metal edge with the already cracked glass—It exploded outward as the tray pushed through the opening leaving a jagged hole. With a chair leg, he broke out the lower points of glass and laid the blanket across the ledge. Placing both hands on the sill, he dove through the space, somersaulting out into the wet shrubs.

Thunder was thankfully still booming, with wind and rain coming in sheets, as Joel recovered from his scratchy fall and darted around the building. Through the shadows of the trees he stumbled and fled, avoiding the security lights, away from the grounds of Global- Tek, as fast as he could go.

He tried to follow the road he remembered leading back to the main highway, ducking out of the way whenever headlights appeared. The white institutional clothing on a running man was itself enough to cause alarm.

Fortunately, the weather with the late time of night worked to his advantage, allowing him to gain some distance. Getting back and clearing his mind was a start, while staying hidden from the authorities was a must—in a world that didn't want the truth.

12

The two men turned their seats to the forward position and connected their seatbelts as the sleek 60XR Learjet descended through the clouds.

"If we had the time, you might enjoy some bone fishing and recreational diving, both popular sports here," said Lucas, gathering and filing his papers inside his leather attaché. He would be glad when his Vatican visitor had departed, and he could get back to his work.

"Wild orchids are more my specialty," said the Jesuit. "Based on my notes, over fifty species have been found on the island."

"Being in the Bermuda Triangle hasn't hurt tourism."

"Or progress below." Father Magruder put his face to the small window.

"The sleeping giant."

"What's that?"

"The nickname for Andros," said Lucas. "Espiritu Santos."

"And that?"

"The name given by the Spanish in 1550."

Andros was the largest and least-explored island in the Bahamas' chain. Stretching over 100 miles from north to south, it was known for its mysterious blue holes, the third largest barrier reef in the world, and its proximity to the Tongue of the Ocean, with depths plunging to over 6,000 feet.

Of more significance to the genetic scientist was the location of a closely guarded undersea US Naval testing facility (AUTEC) at the northeastern corner, through which ultra-top-secret SAP (Special Access Programs) and SCI (Sensitive Compartmental Information) access was granted to the deep sea lab, known as Endor. It had taken months of background checks to clear the priest, with very few clearances approved.

Touchdown at San Andros Airport was smooth. They then taxied to the private hangar where the government car was parked.

"Will wait your call," said the pilot as he shook hands with his parting passengers, the smiling stewardess alongside. The crew was always ready for departure on short notice, motel and restaurant accommodations nearby.

After exchanging greetings, the uniformed driver dropped their bags into the open car trunk, the engine running and ready to go. It was a short drive from the airport at Nicholls Town to the township of Fresh Creek, and to the guarded entrance of AUTEC–The circular logo spelled it out, "Atlantic Undersea Test and Evaluation Center, U.S. Navy".

"Welcome back, Doctor Redding," said the armed military guard, looking inside. "I must check the other visitor's identification and clearance." Magruder handed the papers to him, which he checked and returned. "The Captain is expecting you."

The driver continued through as the gate closed behind, around the gray-block building complex, to a reserved space at the rear wing. After dismissing the driver, Lucas led the way with their bags to the steel security door. A buzzer sounded when they were within a few feet and the door lock released. He pulled it open and they stepped inside.

Commanding Officer Morgan, a U.S. Navy Captain, was just coming out of his private office to greet them.

Lucas did the introductions, "Captain Morgan, Father Magruder from the Vatican. Mac, meet the local commander of AUTEC."

"Any relation to the earlier Captain Morgan?" said Mac after shaking hands. Lucas winced at the query often heard, referencing the 17th century pirate of the Bahamas.

"If I was related to Sir Henry, I wouldn't have a shore billet, Father."

"No gold treasures?"

"None that I've found, but you're welcome to visit his cave at Morgan's Bluff if you've got the time."

"Perhaps another trip," said Lucas. "Is anything else needed for the Navy before we go down?"

"Just the Priest's signature on a liability release and non-disclosure form. We already have yours on file." The document was in his hand, which he put on a table along with a pen. "What you're saying by signing is you understand once you leave the confines of our facility and step from our elevator to Door 54, which is our access to the transfer tunnel, the U.S. Navy is no longer involved or responsible for your safety. Beyond that door, we know nothing. You're completely on your own."

Mac took a moment to scan the form, nodded, and signed.

Only Commander Morgan and Dr. Redding knew, along with the secret overseers, what would happen in the event of a security breach which threatened to expose the project or endanger the Naval facility or others above. Strategic synchronized charges would disconnect and destroy the shuttle sleeve to Endor. Doorways would be sealed and reconfigured. The portal would vanish, as would those who knew of it.

The three walked across the main room into an alcove of elevator doors, to a narrow single-wide service elevator on the end, which the Captain activated with a key. Glances were exchanged but no words were spoken as they stood waiting on the inner humming and precision opening. Then they stepped inside and the doorway vaulted shut with polished steel.

The secure elevator descended the three levels shown on the wall panel and came to a stop. Captain Morgan pulled a knob while inserting and turning a different key. Lucas listened to the whirring sound of gears re-engaging as his eyes adjusted to the red lights of their secondary descent.

"It won't be much longer," said the Captain for the benefit of the first-time visitor. The silver eagle on his khaki collar cast a reddish reflection and reminded Lucas of symbols of past empires and the powers they once heralded. If people only knew.

Soon they came to the final stop and the door opened.

"This is where we part company," said Lucas, leaving the elevator with Mac following.

"Good luck," said Morgan.

The door closed behind them, leaving them in a ten-foot square compartment, bathed in green light. In front was a water-tight door dogged fast with eight handle-levers.

"Here's the most interesting part of the journey," said Lucas, releasing the dog levers one-by-one, then swinging out the heavy metal door. "Climb in behind me."

The transport capsule was like a rolling bullet, with single seats, one in front of the other. After re-dogging the door from inside the transport tube, the two men got into position and locked down the overhead dome.

"How does this thing work?" said Mac.

"Like a ball inside a vacuum hose."

"And how far does this hose carry us?"

"Over a mile. We'll arrive in less than two minutes." Lucas fiddled with the controls which regulated the air flow.

"Whose invention was this, theirs or ours?"

"It was an Admiral's idea, which they implemented and installed, a cooperative venture which they could probably have done better if we had let them handle it alone. But you know how inter-dimensional politics work."

"Under the one-world government, it should go more smoothly," said Mac.

The pressurized air began whistling around the capsule as Lucas raised the vertical flaps and they started to move, quickly gaining speed. Even though the surrounding tube was translucent, the sea was dark at such a depth, so little could be seen until they were closer to Endor.

"Ever wonder why they seem so interested in advancing our weapons technology?" said the Jesuit.

"Not much. Maybe they want to help us defend the planet."

"If we can avoid blowing ourselves up." Mac looked up at a group of lights travelling down from the surface. "Are those what I think?"

"USO.'s on the way to Endor. Their transport is light years ahead of ours."

As the rolling bullet passed the halfway point, a panorama appeared on the bottom of the sea. The two men gazed at the spherical project station sitting like a giant glowing octopus with its appendages spread and pulsating with activity. The clear umbilical cord through which they were riding grew shorter by the second.

Joel rested on the cement incline under a highway overpass, breathing hard after running two miles through a blinding rain. The sound of a siren caused him to push himself further up into the darkness, away from the sweep of car lights. He had no idea he was infringing on someone's spot until a deep voice from behind made his heart jump.

"Just letting you know fellow, you've got company."

"Sorry," Joel replied, "I needed a place to get out of the rain. Didn't know it was taken."

"Don't worry about it. There's enough room." The large bearded man was barely visible. His hand was extended, which Joel shook. "Name's Jake."

"Joel."

"Running from the law?"

"Not exactly."

"Somebody after you?"

"Yeah, the world."

"Sounds like you got problems, bro."

"Big ones. You have no idea."

"You on foot?"

"Not by choice."

"Where headed?"

"Home, I guess."

"Where's that?"

"Green Port, just northeast of here."

"Been through it. Nice beach."

"I've got a place, right on it."

"On the beach? That's cool."

"Yeah, I guess so." Joel wasn't feeling cool, still groggy from the medication.

"Well, I'm heading that way and the rain's letting up. If you don't mind riding between bags in the sidecar, I can give you a lift on my Harley."

"That'd be a huge help." Joel hadn't noticed the motorcycle parked behind one of the cement columns. He quickly followed big Jake. As soon as he had squeezed into the metal compartment, Joel held on as they roared out and up the highway.

In central Florida the rain often fell in patches and it was no surprise to Joel when they soon ran into another heavy shower. There was little choice but to pull off. No overpass, but there was a covered lean-to next to an all-night bar & grill with a flashing OPEN sign.

"Come on in. I'll buy you one," said Jake.

There was hesitation but no resistance to the offer which sounded a pleasurable chord in Joel's memory bank. He was tired, frustrated at society, and frankly worn down, not about to turn down such kindness and hope of relief.

Inside, a sleepy-looking bartender shifted his eyes in their direction while dispensing a draft, then slid the mug to his lone customer who was staring up at a talk show through furls of cigarette smoke. It was a blue-lit bar with plenty of empty stools, built like a horseshoe against a liquor-bottle wall, beer taps at each bend and a cloudy jar of pickled pig's feet at one end.

As they claimed a couple stools, the repeated dings of a pinball machine and the racking of pool balls could be heard in the red-lit area behind them.

"You guys want some music?" It was a woman's voice causing Joel to turn. She had heavy make-up, piled up platinum hair, and a what-have-we-here look. The quarter in her hand was resting against the juke box.

"Whatcha think, buddy?" said Jake with a glint of amusement.

"Go for it if you like," said Joel.

"Is that a yes?" said the beer-room doll.

"No thanks," said Joel, averting her gaze.

"Bring us a couple Bud drafts," said Jake to the bartender who was wiping the area in front of them.

"A pitcher's cheaper, if you're having more than one."

"Sure. Bring it on." Jake slapped a twenty on the bar.

With his first couple of beers, Joel felt a twinge of guilt and a flashback to sad times, but not enough to slow him down. Big Jake had some jokes and interesting tales. Soon Joel was able to loosen up and laugh, even more with the second pitcher and a few shots. The platinum chick with raccoon eyes was swirling with herself in the pulsating lights to the crooning of Elvis. Then something shifted within Joel. Life was no longer funny. He remembered stuff that upset him, things people had said and done, and ways they had looked at him. He thought of Amber. Where was she?

Why was he here wasting his time? "Let's go," said Joel.

Big Jake stopped as he was lifting another drink and set it sharply down on the bar. "You're right. We need to get back on the road." He reached for his wallet to settle.

Joel staggered on outside. The whine of a dog caught his attention. It was a chocolate lab with his nose pressed against a pick-up window, reminding him of Midnight. Poor animal, just wanted to get out, a little freedom. Without thinking, Joel reached for the door handle and pulled it open allowing the dog to escape. In the pocket of the open door was a gun.

He grabbed it, stuffed it in his waistline, and joined Jake on his way out.

With a rumble the Harley was back on the highway heading north in the direction of Green Port. The rain had passed, and stars were visible. There was barely any traffic so early, even as they got closer to town. Using hand signals, Joel directed Jake to the place where he planned to go, and it wasn't the beach. He was still dizzy even after breathing the cool night air but managed to climb out of the sidecar.

"Hey, my big man, thanks for the lift, and the drinks." Joel gave Jake a pat on the back of his leather jacket.

"Sure, bro. Anytime. Stay cool." With a roar, big Jake took off.

Joel trudged up the grassy slope, past the sign that read, "Beaches Animal Clinic," and through the bushes that bordered the building.

Sun beams refracted through the broken window into the office of Veterinarian Doctor Leslie Lane. Seated behind his desk was an unshaven man dressed like a chain-gang escapee, waiting with a gun.

There was a jingling sound of keys at the door. Joel's eyes popped open. He gripped and raised the pistol. With the anger he was feeling, it didn't matter to him how he got the truth. Like a lion, he would start by paralyzing his prey with fear. The door slowly opened, and the Doctor appeared, looking the way Joel had wanted.

"Step inside and close the door," said Joel, rising from his seat.

"If it's drugs or money, I can– "

"Shut up. It's neither." Joel forced the Doctor to sit down in his office chair, and then pressed the gun to the back of his head.

"Please don't shoot. Whatever you want, I'll give you."

"Tell me, why did you have Amber arrested?"

"Who sent you?"

"Nobody. Amber Wells is a friend of mine, and she doesn't do drugs."

"If I tell anyone, they'll destroy my business."

"If you don't, you won't be around to run it." Joel pressed harder with the pistol.

"Don't shoot. Okay. You're right." "She didn't steal the drugs?"

"Why did you charge her?"

"I didn't want to. They threatened me and made me do it. Believe me they have the power."

"Who are they?"

"A super intelligence-they knew of the discovery, and much more."

"What discovery?"

"A jawbone she brought in for me to identify."

"What was it?"

"I tried to find out, even called the Smithsonian. They wanted to help but needed the bone."

"Why did they want her arrested?"

"Maybe because she had the fossil they wanted. I was trying to hold it for them."

"Where did they take her?"

"Prison, I guess."

"She's not in any prison."

"I really don't know."

"You're not any help. You can't tell me anything."

"Listen. Please put down the gun and I will help you

Joel withdrew the gun a few inches. "Go ahead, but it better be fast." He needed to leave before others arrived at the clinic.

Lines of concentration glistened with sweat on the Doctor's forehead as he spoke, "When I first examined the bone and saw the skeleton photo on Amber's phone, I knew it was a scientific find of immense significance. Then I made some calls."

"Go on."

"My usual fossil contacts were not much help, so I called the Smithsonian. There I was redirected and transferred several times until I finally got someone who seemed to know what I was describing. He told me that it was highly important that I hold on to the fossil, that it stayed here until they could come and examine it themselves."

"Did they come?"

"Amber got it. Didn't give them time."

"How does that help me?"

"Find the bone and maybe you'll find Amber."

"I'm running out of patience. How can you help me do that?"

"Listen. I suspected after first speaking with them by phone that such a discovery needed some insurance against loss; so, the evening I had the fossil, I planted a chip. I didn't tell anyone."

"What are you saying?"

"There's a GPS tracking chip concealed between two teeth in the jawbone."

Joel slowly lowered his weapon. "You know where it is?"

"The signal was lost."

Without comment, Joel raised the pistol.

"It went dead, but I can give you the last coordinates."

"Where is that?"

"A hundred and seventy miles off the Florida coast– Andros Island. Here, I've written down the last recorded position." The Doctor pulled a slip of paper from his desk drawer and handed it to Joel who looked at the figures.

"Latitude 24.747178, Longitude 77.810422"–It wasn't what he wanted, but it was better than nothing.

"I pulled it up on the computer. It's one of the island's blue holes called, The Guardian."

"What size pants you wear?"

"Thirty-six. Why?"

"Take 'em off. Shirt too. We're trading."

In a few minutes Joel had swapped clothes with Leslie Lane. Leaving the office, he walked past a red-haired receptionist busy straightening her desk. Noticing her name plate, he said, "Have a wonderful day, Betty."

"Thank you, Doc—"

13

Amber cringed from the feel of the scaly finger tracing its way down the side of her neck, across her shoulder and exploring the bones of her arm. The hope of waking from a terrible dream was gone. Memories of walking on the beach with her dog, working at the clinic with the animals, sailing through the surf with Joel, were all just that–they couldn't come back.

She had no idea where she was or how she had gotten there. Her surroundings reminded her of a kennel, but in the place of cages there were glass bubbles, and looking through them were humans, being maintained by tubes. Creatures from her living nightmare were moving around, probing and staring at their captives, as in a reverse zoo, with their elongated eyes inches away, smelling of sulfur. There was one that tried the staring thing on Amber while lifting her bubble. Amber spit on it. The little mouth widened baring a set of nasty pointed teeth, and then it wandered off finding a more cooperative subject.

None of the creatures spoke audibly, perhaps communicating among themselves telepathically; so, when Amber heard a human voice, she strained to hear every word.

"This area is called our harvest room." "Very suitable," said a man.

"Yes, the work is on target." Amber recognized that one, known as the Doctor.

"All cooperative?"

"Eventually."

"Drugs?"

"Usually mind control."

"This one?" Amber knew she was the subject.

"A recent arrival."

"She looks more alert than the others."

"She'll fit in, but we may have to use drugs."

"How long do they last?"

"It depends on the implant. Severe cramping and bloating can occur following embryo transfer, and worse."

"Can we visit the hatchery?"

"If you have the fortitude," said the Doctor, directing his guest to the door.

Amber thought of appealing to the visitor for help, but kept her mouth shut. She couldn't conceive of where any help might come from. Fortunately for now her follicles weren't ready for harvesting. As for an implant, she had seen the huge syringe employed on others and dreaded the thought of it, unable to imagine the birthing of whatever it was being implanted in the human hosts.

Waiting and watching the things happening around her was distressing, but something deeper stirred Amber's soul as she closed her eyes. A vision emerged of a time in her childhood, at age eleven, while living in a small South Georgia town.

It was a Saturday morning, in a trailer on a dirt road. There was a knock and her mother went to the door. It was a nice-looking man wearing a tie, and another standing on the steps. They had come from a local church and wanted to share something from a little booklet.

Mother thanked them and said that she already belonged to a church, but Amber cracked the door and peeked out. The nice man asked if he could share the booklet with her. Mother gave permission, so she stepped out onto the open wooden porch. She sat on the edge as he stood on the ground going through the pages with her.

The booklet was about God and His love for her, and His Son who died in her place for her sins, then rose from the dead. Amber prayed asking Jesus to come into her heart and wiped her cheek as a tear rolled down.

She never went to the nice man's church, though invited, and as she got older, forgot the warm and wonderful feeling she experienced that day. Later with other party-loving friends, she scoffed at the religious people for the narrow-minded rules they followed. She wanted freedom to do things they wouldn't approve, like reading her horoscope, smoking a cigarette, and sneaking out at night to have fun.

Now she felt a deep sense of sorrow and shame for turning her back on God, ignoring the One who had brought her such joy and peace as a child. In her vision she saw the Ouija board she had looked to for guidance, and the planchette moving across the letters, down to the word–GOODBYE.

"I'm so sorry, Jesus," Amber breathed within the bubble. "Please forgive me."

Joel pushed open the chapel trailer door, wondering if he had made a wise move by going to Chaplain Simon. There was no-one else he could begin to trust at this point.

"We need to talk."

Simon got up from his chair and walked past Joel to the door, turned the lock and changed the window sign from OPEN to CHAPLAIN OFF DUTY. "For an armed and dangerous fugitive from an asylum, you don't seem dressed the part."

"You've heard?"

"Alerts have been hitting the phone every hour. Coffee? Food?"

"I could use both."

"Have a seat. Sounds like you have a lot to talk about."

Joel settled into a chair and took a deep breath, relaxing a little for the first time. Soon he had drink and a sandwich, and in his mind, started trying to process all the events and the best way to convey them to convince Simon of the truth.

"Would you like to start with the gun?" said Simon.

"Don't worry. I ditched it on the way here from the Animal Clinic."

"Did you use it?"

"You better believe it." Joel paused, looking Simon in the eyes. "And I might've pulled the trigger, but he talked."

"Who talked?"

"The veterinarian who fabricated the drug-theft charges against Amber."

"They were false?"

"I knew it all along. She wasn't hooked on drugs."

"Have you been drinking?" It was still on Joel's breath and in his countenance.

"Yeah, I relapsed. A guy gave me a ride. We stopped in the rain at a bar and grill. He bought. It's where I picked up the pistol."

"And the clothes?"

"Compliments of Doctor Lane."

"Why did he charge Amber?"

"It gets deep."

"Go ahead. I'm listening."

"It all goes back to that fossil we found on the beach that looked like a mermaid..." Joel continued to fill in Simon with a replay of all the details, the mysterious evacuation of the skeleton, his encounters with the renowned geneticist, and the jawbone lost then re-found with Redding's stuff at the Donnelly estate. "They said Amber was arrested, but I couldn't locate her anywhere. They forcibly committed me and tried their best to brainwash me, to keep me from remembering what I had seen." Joel paused to give Simon time to take in what he was saying. "I'm not a conspiracy theorist, just a small-town reporter, not looking for trouble. You understand?"

"It's complicated, but I'm still listening." Simon was taking small sips of his coffee.

"I know what I've been through, and this thing is highly coordinated. I'm not lying."

"I never said you were."

"Doctor Lane was threatened to produce the fossil. When Amber took it, he had to press charges. All this time we were told it was nothing but a sea cow."

"Why would anyone risk so much to get the bones of a sea cow?"

"Exactly. It had to be something more, which Dr. Lane knew. That's why he chipped it."

"Chipped?"

"He hid a miniature GPS tracking device inside the jawbone, wanting to keep up with it; and since it disappeared the same time as Amber—"

"They may be together? Did he tell you where?"

"He gave me the last coordinates, which leaves us in a blue hole on Andros Island. That's where the signal stopped.

Simon was deep in thought.

"You probably don't believe half of all this," said Joel.

"I believe it, more than you know." To Simon, the conspiracy theorists merely scratched the surface. If they knew the truth about the workings of their real enemy, they would all be on their knees in prayer. "The whole world lies in the lap of the evil one—Satan—the god of this world system, the prince of the power of the air. The Bible reveals it. Yes, Joel, we're in a battle and most of it is invisible."

"I'm a reporter, not a fiction writer."

"You've seen enough to know a little."

"Yeah, and I don't like it one bit."

"You think I do?"

"You're a minister."

"Still learning to fight better."

"Teach me."

"As we go along."

"I'm ready to start. We need to find Amber."

"Lesson one, don't rush into battle without your armor on."

"Armor?"

"Ephesians Six. Let's pray it on."

Simon took them by prayer into the heavenly realms, into the throne-room of grace and presence of the Holy God of Creation, through the Blood and the Name that is above every name, the LORD of lords and KING of kings, Jesus Christ. His faith request was for wisdom, protection and direction.

As they waited for guidance, the journey became clear. It was a reaffirming of the revelation given to Simon earlier by the truck driver.

Simon went into the back room and brought out some clothes, tossing them to Joel. "Better change into something that will blend in better with the island locals."

While Joel made the exchange, Simon made a call to an old friend named Ron, in the boating business, about thirty miles south. As was often the case when being Divinely directed, favor was on their side. Text alerts of the escaped and armed mental patient were still showing up on Simon's phone.

After packing some food and water, the two headed out of Green Port in his old pick-up headed south. They weren't going to risk stopping along the way with the probability of Joel's face being posted on TV and in local papers.

"You said that God told you about this trip ahead of time?" said Joel.

"Not everything, just that I was to go with you."

"How does that work? Do you actually hear a voice?"

"Not audibly, but I know what He's saying."

"What if He tells you to do something crazy?"

"If you know Him, you know He's not crazy. He's got everything figured out. And there's no safer place to be than obedient."

"Changing the subject, do you mind if I ask if you're married?"

"Not yet, but we do have plans when she returns from her missionary work in Guatemala. What about you and Amber? Given it any prayer?"

"Nothing serious."

"Enjoy spending time with her?"

"You could say that."

"This trip is pretty serious."

"Yeah."

"From what you've told me, it could be deadly."

Silence.

"How do you feel about dying?"

"It is what it is."

"That's an easy thing to say, but are you ready?"

Silence.

"Joel, if God were to ask you why He should let you into His perfect place called Heaven, what would you say?"

"Hey, I could say I'm a friend of Simon Johnson."

Simon smiled. "That much is true, but our friendship couldn't help you with that."

"I went to church as a child."

"Same story. The church can't help you there."

"I'm not that bad."

"How much bad should God let into heaven?"

Silence.

"Friend, I've been in your shoes. I know what you're feeling – a little angry and confused, right?"

"You got it." Joel was watching the trees race by.

"You want the peace and assurance that comes from being fully forgiven and accepted by your Father in heaven.

"How is that possible?"

"Because of what His Son did for you."

"The cross?"

"That's what it took—a sinless sacrifice to pay in full for your sins and mine. Jesus bore our sins in His Body. He bought us with His Blood."

"It makes no sense."

"It's God's love and God's only way for man to be saved from judgment."

"Where does that leave me?"

"Do you want to pay for your own sins and miss heaven?"

"No. I need what you have."

"There's a rest stop just ahead. Let me help you settle this issue with God for good."

Simon slowed and took the exit, pulling into a shaded space away from the other parked cars. Joel's heart was racing, part of him still resisting this decision to do what was needed. As Simon calmly and clearly showed him from God's Word man's sin problem and God's solution, like a seed it began to take hold. It was the only thing in life that mattered. He wanted his Father's love and acceptance more than anything.

When the time came to pray, Joel felt a deep sorrow that his sins required the suffering and death of God's own

Son. The words poured out of his mouth, "Dear Lord Jesus, how can I ever thank you enough for what you have done for me, dying to take away all my sins. Please forgive me and cleanse me. Come into my heart. Give me what Simon's got."

Joel then felt Simon's hand on his shoulder along with his prayer, "Father, impart your Holy Spirit of the risen Lord Jesus Christ to Joel now, with your righteousness, peace and joy. Thank you, Lord."

He lifted his tear-streaked face and felt different, lighter, as a terrible load had been taken away. A new awareness had come, a peaceful presence like nothing he had ever before experienced.

"Do you realize what has just happened?" asked Simon.

"I'm forgiven."

"And born again, spiritually, a new creation in Christ Jesus. The angels in heaven are rejoicing."

"Awesome. Why did I wait so long? Everybody should do this."

"How true. Now you can tell others." "And start reading the Bible."

"With understanding."

After a few more minutes of quiet, Simon cranked up his truck and they pulled back out on the highway. *Some rest stop*, thought Joel.

"Better grab a sandwich from the cooler," said Simon. "You may not feel like eating on the boat."

"Me? I do some sailing," said Joel, reaching around the seat for some food and drink which he set in the console.

"A cigarette is a different experience."

"Cigarettes? I gave them up."

"Just the trade name for go-fast boats, the kind Ron deals with."

After a while Simon recognized the exit and left the main highway heading due east for the coast. In five miles they turned onto a narrow dirt and gravel road, then passed through a tunnel of palms, between some tall metal storage sheds, and finally to an open area with wooden docks and boats—one on a lift, two on the bank and others in the water. Several men were involved in various activities.

Simon parked alongside the weathered dock-house. A brass bell hung on the outside wall with words painted above, RING FOR RON. He reached for the rope and jerked the clapper. The loud clang was enough to turn the workers' heads, and in a moment a man's deep voice was heard from inside, "Hang on. Be right out."

Sure enough, the screen door banged and out stepped the main man of Hawaii Five-O, moustache and flowery shirt to prove it. A big belly and broad smile seemed perfect for the part.

"How's my ol' buddy," said Ron, giving Simon a bear hug. "Who's your friend?"

"Finer than frog hair," said Simon. "Meet Joel, the one who needs our help."

"My pleasure to finally meet you," said Joel, shaking Ron's hand.

"You guys got your gear?"

"We're ready."

"Grab your stuff and let's go. I've got a boat delivery in Nassau and will drop you two off at Small Hope Marina at Andros on the way."

Simon re-parked the truck, they got their things, and proceeded with Ron to the end of the main dock where a man was standing next to a long, open-cockpit boat.

"It's all checked out, boss," said the worker, "full tank."

The rumbling of engines could be heard from the stern waterline, reminding Joel of racehorses waiting for the gate to lift.

"This one's a beauty," said Ron, checking it stem to stern. "A thirty-eight Top Gun loaded with twin 750 inboard Mercs. We're talking 110 miles-per-hour top end on a smooth sea. Probably will have to keep it around 80 today. A little choppy."

"How long do you expect the trip to take?" said Simon, stepping into the go-fast, then taking the gear from Joel who quickly followed.

"The chart shows 229 nautical miles, which is roughly two and a half to three hours if you know how to pray."

"Glad to know you still do," said Simon.

"A rough sea can break a sailor fast. You two grab the lines." The dockhand had already released the bow line and was loosening the remaining stern line, ready to toss it clear of the engine action. "Take in the lines." As the bow swung out, Ron nudged both throttles forward. Simon was in the port bolster seat while Ron stood at the starboard controls with his hand on the wheel. The sudden forward motion caught Joel by surprise and helped him down into the rear bench seat. There was a light breeze as they headed away from the dock and into the channel that led to the open ocean. Joel was taking it all in.

After clearing the last red and green channel markers, Captain Ron looked around at his two-man cargo with a mischievous expression and said, "Ready?"

Simon looked back at Joel with raised eyebrows. "You're the captain," said Joel. "We're along for the ride."

"Don't worry, I trained with a modified go-fast as a Navy Seal. Love these things." While he spoke, Joel watched Ron's arms straighten against both throttles. There was an instant surge with the thundering crescendo of the twin Mercs churning the surf. He quickly realized why go-fast passengers don't wear caps as the relative wind multiplied in force.

"Unbelievable," Joel breathed, as he felt the light-weight fiber craft skim over the surface barely bumping the waves. He spotted the digital controls that showed the speed and saw it climb to 80, 85, 90, and beyond. He turned back to note the rapidly vanishing shoreline being enveloped in a sky and sea wash of blues. God was gracious to toss some excitement into the mix, he thought, even while his heart ached for Amber's safety.

14

Lucas Redding placed his hand under the scanner. As the green light blinked, the titanium doors slowly retracted. He felt uneasy revealing the contents of the rooms to outsiders, realizing that knowledge gives power; but the influence of the Vatican had prevailed. Both groups had their secrets and one day the favor of access might be returned.

"Be careful not to touch any of the bones. Contamination of the structures has to be rigidly controlled."

"I wouldn't think of it," said the Jesuit, following closely into a dimly lit passageway which soon opened into a large area.

"Exhibit One. Lights." Redding's voice command activated the illumination. "What you are seeing we call *Dawn of Legends.*"

"An intriguing designation." Magruder took a step back, his eyes rolling up and down the twenty-seven foot human-like skeleton, from the giant skull to the massive rib cage, past the long arms and legs to the splays of six fingers and six toes—all so huge that it could barely be contained in the display chamber. It was a typical first-time response.

"Quite a jump from the nine to twelve-footers collected by the Smithsonian," said Redding.

"Antediluvian Nephilim—the fallen ones' ancient progeny. I had imagined them from Enoch's writings, but had not heard of any being recovered."

"By orders we conceal it, as we do the worldwide deluge," said Lucas, as if affirming loyalty.

"Of course. Such knowledge could stir resistance."

"Wait till you see the others." Lucas turned and led the way from the first chamber through the corridor into a second, not quite as large. "Exhibit two. Lights."

"Greek mythology? Right?" Mac was entranced by the skeletal body of a horse, joined to the torso, arms and head of a man—a Centaur.

"The unthinking masses have no idea."

"The legends are re-dawning."

"With some genetic help—as in the days of Noah."

"You can do that with gene splicing?" Mac was exploring but Lucas felt no obligation to say more.

"The Watchers had their ways. Shall we continue?" said Redding, ushering his guest on through the passageway and into the third chamber. "Exhibit three. Lights."

"Mother Mary, what is it?"

"An avian transhuman, or bird-man as some call them."

The bones were human in form except for its beaked falcon-head, and hands at the ends of its wings. It stood over six feet tall with a wingspan of ten and had the tail of a peacock.

"Ancient Egypt," said Mac, closely studying it all around.

"They also appear in petroglyphs and cave paintings—just wild imagination. Right?"

"Of course. Why terrify humanity before the time? How on earth did you obtain such an artifact?"

"Once we learn of such a thing, we spare no power or expense to remove it from public awareness," said the scientist, looking the Jesuit in the eyes, "which sometimes requires a clean-up." Understanding registered.

"To my knowledge these kinds have never been found."

"It's best that you believe that. We have one more chamber."

The fourth and final display room was no larger than the previous two, with fifteen-foot ceilings and slightly lifted staging platforms. "Exhibit four. Lights."

"My, my," said Mac. "This makes me miss our Starbucks. You're sure this isn't a hoax?"

"Why waste time on hoaxes when we have the real thing?"

"Just kidding. The Vatican also knows of these creatures."

"A merman, or from your Greek mythology, a triton, son of Poseidon and Amphitrite."

"Lucas, I must say you know your stuff."

"You should hear them play conch shells."

"Entrancing?"

"We'll view some shortly."

Mac scrutinized the skeletal anatomy with the upper body of a human and lower structure of a fish. The jawbone was back in place. Upon scanning it, Lucas had discovered an implanted tracking device which he hastily destroyed and kept secret, fearing possible repercussions from the powers.

Before continuing with the Jesuit into areas of hybrid research and development, there was a matter that needed addressing concerning a piece of religious jewelry that had been offensive to the overseers—not a big thing.

Magruder reacted with some surprise, "The cross?"

"Mac, religion is your area. Mine is science. But haven't you noticed the way they react around you?"

"It's just part of our attire."

"The overseers registered a grievance."

"I honestly hadn't noticed."

"Would it be a problem to pocket it?"

The Jesuit unclipped the cross and slipped it into his pants pocket. "Anything to keep the peace."

Lucas remembered a painful childhood incident, when he once attended what had been described as a rock concert. It turned out to be a Christian thing, and they were handing out stuff. Lucas tried wearing the wooden cross on a string. As soon as his buddies saw it, they ridiculed him for his foolishness. He yanked it from his neck and threw it into the trash. Never again, he vowed.

The aqua bay and white sands shoreline dotted with tropical palms and mangos should have been relaxing to Joel, given his attraction to such surroundings, but the Bahamian island presented a challenge with only a set of coordinates as a clue. Andros stretched 104 miles long by 40 miles wide. They were finally arriving. Ron powered down the 38-foot fast boat easing through the crystal blue bay waters, motoring up alongside the end of a long stationary dock where they secured a couple of lines for Joel and Simon to step ashore with their bags.

"Welcome to Small Hope Bay, cradle of the sleeping giant," said the islander with a beaming smile and orange shirt. He had been waiting on the dock for their arrival.

"Joel and Simon, meet Phillip, the best part-Seminole guide and blue hole diver on Andros Island," said Ron. "He will take good care of you."

After the initial greeting and a few parting words of appreciation, the two passengers tossed the lines back to Ron and watched as the sleek go-fast rumbled away on its way to Nassau. They then picked up their stuff and headed up the dock to the nearby lodge where Joel had made reservations. They agreed to meet Phillip in the restaurant following their check-in and brief visit to their bay side cabin. It was small but adequate, of limestone and pine construction.

The outside dining patio was where the three decided to sit.

"My good boating friend tells me that you can use some special help in exploring our island," said Phillip, taking a gulp of mango juice.

"We can," said Simon. "First, I'm curious to know how Small Hope Bay got its name."

"Certainly, you have read of the early pirate, Captain Henry Morgan."

"Yes, I have," said Simon.

"The story is that he buried quite a stash of treasure somewhere on this island, and proudly boasted that anyone would have small hope of ever finding it; and to this date no one has."

"This place was a home for pirates?" said Simon.

"If you like, we can visit Morgan's Bluff."

"Interesting," said Joel, "but the history lesson will have to wait for another trip."

"No problem," said Phillip. "There is much more to do and see on our big island."

Joel and Simon both paused to take a bite of their fish sandwiches.

"You like my shirt? Androsia Batik, made in factory right here, many colors and prints. We can go see."

They were still chewing.

"Or birds? Andros is home to over 200 species—the Bahama Oriole, the Great Lizard Cuckoo, the rare Kirtland's Warbler, the Piping Plover, the West Indian Whistling Duck, and many others can be spotted."

Both took another bite.

"Maybe you like to fish. Bone fishing is fun. I can take you to our famous reef. Any kind of fish you like, I can find for you."

"What about the Naval base?" said Joel.

Phillip tilted his head.

"Can you give us a tour?" Joel felt that the undersea test center might be a good starting place in their search.

"It is sometimes open to visitors. We can see. I make no promise." Phillip didn't seem comfortable with their choice, but at least was willing to try.

Island transportation came in colorful varieties on bicycles, scooters and cars. Phillip's was an old VW camping van which he had painted to the hilt.

"Hop aboard the happy bus," said Phillip in his welcoming way. As soon as Joel and Simon were seated, he closed the door and assumed the place of tour-guide, talking while driving. "Cold drinks are in the electric cooler. Please help yourselves."

They puttered north on the Queen's Highway and listened to Phillip describe the Island—its early Seminole and African slave settlements, Spanish and British rule, topography and geological formations. "All the main islands of the Bahamas have blue holes, but here we have many more, 178 on land and at least fifty off-shore."

"What are they?" said Joel.

"Blue holes are entrances to incredible cave systems that run below the Island to the sea floor."

"I've seen a film on them by Cousteau," said Simon.

"He did some exploring," said Phillip. "Divers from National Geographic have also come and filmed. But there is much more still to be found."

"Isn't there a local legend of a sea monster?" said Simon.

"It's called the Lusca," said Phillip, "reported to be over seventy-five feet in length. Cave divers go missing every year. Andros natives don't call it legend."

Their conversation was cut short by their arrival at the secured gates of a concrete walled facility. Joel quickly saw movement and the emergence of a man in uniform. The two passengers waited while Phillip stepped out and met the guard who appeared tense. They watched as Phillip gestured. After some minutes the guard made a call on his phone, a pass was handed to Phillip, and the gate slowly opened.

"You got us in," said Joel.

"No problem," said Phillip. "The happy bus takes you everywhere."

"How?" asked Simon.

"I know the man's brother. Promised them some crabs."

"Crabs to get into a Naval base?"

"Most delicious, our island crabs. But we can't stay long. It is a restricted pass."

With a military wave from the guard, they drove through the gate which closed behind them, then followed an asphalt drive approved for visitors as diagramed on the back of the pass. There wasn't much to see but some scattered single-level buildings, storage units, a forklift and a few government vehicles. Joel saw few people.

"How did the U.S. Navy happen to get here?" said Simon.

Phillip pulled the van in next to a hangar-type structure, then picked up a brochure. "Let me read this part—

"A joint United States–United Kingdom agreement signed in 1963 with the concurrence of the Bahamian government, enabled the United States to develop this area of water and certain territory on the east coast of Andros Island, readily accessible to the TOTO– "

"TOTO?" interrupted Simon.

"The Tongue of The Ocean is a deep-ocean basin approximately 100 miles long by 15 miles wide, plunging as deep as 6,000 feet–ideal for testing submarine capabilities."

"Thanks for the info," said Joel. He noticed an opening at the side of the hangar and slid open the van door to step out for a look inside.

"What's happening, my friend?" said Phillip with alarm in his voice.

"Just taking a quick peek at what's inside," said Joel. Simon followed.

"Hey, mon. Restricted pass means staying in bus." Phillip's words were lost as the two made their way to the partly open hangar door.

Joel looked inside first and felt his heart leap. Occupying the center of the hangar was a camouflage-painted amphibious vehicle, like a past dream springing to life. "Just like it."

"Just like what?" said Simon, sharing the opening.

"Just like what I saw on the beach at Green Port."

There were other large covered objects that drew him in for a closer look.

"Hey, someone's coming!" said Simon, pulling on Joel's shirt. "The sign says RESTRICTED AREA."

Phillip was standing outside the van, arms raised, as two guards approached with trained weapons. Joel and Simon were quickly surrounded, and the Officer on Duty was summoned.

They wisely played the part of dumb tourists with deep apology. After a battery of questions, examination of identification, and a stern lecture on public rules and restrictions, the three were released from custody and the happy bus was directly escorted to the exit gate. "Sorry to do this to you, Phillip," said Joel from the back.

"No problem, mon. Nothing crabs can't fix."

Later, back in their cabin, Joel retold the story to Simon of the beach invasion with seizure of the skeleton and their return into the sea.

"I just don't see how you can be sure it's the same one," said Simon. "Any military facility on the water could have an amphibious vehicle."

"How many military units are based directly off the Florida coast?"

"Can't say I know of any others."

"And in close proximity to the coordinates of the missing fossil?"

"You may have something–an incomplete skeleton being rejoined with its jaw."

"Both point to Andros," said Joel.

There was a tap on the door. It was Phillip, with a nautical chart in his hands, who had returned to discuss plans for the next day. They had to check the coordinates Joel had gotten from the veterinarian.

Carefully locating the latitude and longitude figures, Phillip marked the chart with a cross. "It's the main entrance of the Guardian, one of the deepest blue holes in the Bahamas."

"How far away?" said Joel.

"About forty-minutes' drive, and a five-minute walk through the brush."

"You've been in it before?" said Simon.

"Twice, through part of it. Some parts that tunnel to the ocean are still unexplored."

"Captain Ron said you're the man to take us down," said Joel. "Will you do it?"

"Cave diving is the most dangerous sport on earth," said Phillip, rolling up the chart. "Are you both certified?"

Fortunately, both Simon and Joel had certifications from previous diving.

"We'll be ready."

"I'll have all the gear together here in the morning—suits, tanks, lights, guide-line, everything we need."

15

The hexagon room at the center of Endor was the deep-sea site for high level meetings. It was where Dr. Lucas Redding received directives for his transgenetic work and presented reports on his achievements. The cold sterility of the gray metal surroundings served to remind him of the calibrated precision expected by the powers, and the intolerance held toward any workers who strayed from their orders. He was satisfied to stay in line, being well rewarded financially for his contributions.

Lucas had been notified of the special meeting an hour earlier. It was midnight and he was seated opposite the Jesuit priest, Magruder, who was scheduled to return to Rome in the morning. Also seated around the hexagonal table were three others, reptilian area rulers, all waiting for the head power to arrive.

Mac appeared unsettled by the attention he was getting from the one next to him.

"You are a priest?"

Mac nodded.

"What can you do for us?"

"Bless you, my brother. The Roman Catholic Church extends its universal hand to all God's creatures."

"Can you give us powers?"

"I operate under Papal authority and am honored to inform you that the Pontiff has approved baptism of extraterrestrials, which surely includes beings such as yourselves. We can discuss it further on my next visit."

Attention immediately turned to the head chair and the manifestation of the leader, preceded by the familiar wing flaps. Lucas watched Mac's eyes widen with the sudden appearance of the imposing angelic dark power with his wing crests and pointed ears, pitch black with the face of a man revealing lines of cunning and craftiness.

"Welcome to Endor, Jesuit Magruder. You seem surprised to see me."

"It's uncanny how much you resemble the figure the media portrays as batman," said Magruder.

"Correction—How little their puny portrayal resembles me. But how they do adore me with all their dark adornment and hero worship."

Father Mac was silent.

"I existed long before the modern media, and fully understand human manipulation. Darkness has an attraction to most. Don't you agree, or am I turning your theology upside down?"

"It's true."

"Isn't it fitting that an angel with bat DNA, such as myself, would be placed in charge of transgenetic preparations for global transformation? You don't need to answer or be too concerned. The Vatican will be granted worldwide religious rule if cooperation continues. As you know, Islam is also vying for the reins."

"We will cooperate," said the priest.

"As expected. Has Lucas given you an adequate tour?"

"Quite."

"As it was in the days of Noah?"

"Very close."

"Do our rulers have their areas on schedule?"

All three reptilians nodded. If they had not, thought Lucas, they would have been replaced before morning light.

The powerful angel suddenly turned, fully facing Lucas, as a bat homing in on a moth. "Now, for a matter of housekeeping, I must deal with an issue involving one of our overseers, Dr. Lucas Redding." Pause. "Lucas, I trusted you with a key element of our operations and have compensated you far above your peers. You, more than the others, should know the importance of preventing outsiders from holding transgenic fossils. In the wrong hands it threatens to undermine the uniformitarian story of earth history which represents a large element of our control."

Redding was feeling like the moth.

"Following the Green Port incident, we took care of the woman and expected you to take care of the man. You assured us it was done, that he was neutralized within the Global-Tek facilities. Did you know that he escaped?"

Lucas swallowed hard, without comment. This was alarming news. He was starting to feel the panic of the pursued moth, unable to shake its predator.

"Not only has he escaped, but this one, Joel Landon, has somehow followed you to Andros Island. His identity was just scanned by a guard at AUTEC."

The pain of the unforeseen attack felt certain. All eyes in the hexagon were on him. His survival depended on what he might say at this moment, as the moth's life was spared by the last-minute secretion of a defensive liquid. "Let me first applaud our leader on his intelligence and efficiency," said Lucas, looking around the table. "I have patterned my management of this situation as I would expect our leader to have done, given the circumstances. What better place to have your opponent than within your own domain?"

"Very well, Doctor. Do what you need to do, but know that we are carefully watching. Absolutely no more mistakes."

Legends usually have a basis of truth to their origin—such had been the studied conclusion Joel had drawn from tribal stories worldwide that paralleled ancient historical records. But considering the Lusca monster within the blue holes of Andros Island, said to be part shark and part octopus, 200-feet in length, Joel was extremely dubious. Although he did see how such stories might affect divers breathing rates and jeopardize their safety within tight and unfamiliar passages.

The morning sky was clear blue with just one plane, a jet, making a climbing turn eastward on a transatlantic flight. The main entrance pond to the Guardian Blue Hole looked yellowish-green to Joel who stood suited up along with Simon and their diving guide, Phillip.

"I thought these holes were supposed to be blue," said Joel.

"This one's got some hydrogen sulfide near the surface, but will clear below ninety feet," said Phillip, "Remember to stay close and follow the guidelines."

"Have you ever had to use the bail-out bottles?" Simon was referring to the mini cylinders of oxygen holstered to their waists.

"Only once when a regulator stopped working, but this is all new equipment. We shouldn't have any problems."

Joel didn't envision any such problems but needed more than just a safe dive. He needed to discover a clue to the disappearance of the jawbone in this spot, and hopefully learn what happened to Amber. They had prayed before leaving the cabin.

Flippers on, flashlights activated and breathing masks down, the three divers dropped in from the rocky border and lined up to follow the leader. The first guideline had already been placed by a past dive team and would take them a certain distance before a new line was needed.

Joel trailed, one hand on the line and kept the other on his light which was required from the start. Ten feet ahead, Phillip began fading from sight in the cloudy sulfurous water and Simon was barely visible from behind.

Phillip slowed down enough to allow Joel to keep him in sight while shifting his light around to see where he was going. Except for the lights, everything was ink-black below. The yellow-green glow from the surface gradually diminished.

As they continued their descent, Joel recalled the feelings he had as a child while hiding between clothes in his parents' closet, how quiet it was with no movement of air, with no sounds or stimuli of anything else in the world. Going into a dark-water cave was like that, the most movement being the regulated release of bubbles coming from their tanks.

Once below the bands of sediment, Joel found it easier to see. As he fin-kicked along between Phillip and Simon, their light beams pierced further into the darkness revealing craggy recesses and holes like giant swiss cheese. Rocky protrusions cast shape-shifting shadows playing with Joel's imagination as they moved through both wide and narrow passages. Under ninety feet the water cleared like glass and a blue-green spectrum of colors began to emerge as the cavern opened to a panorama of hanging stalactites and rising floor formations.

Phillip stopped at the end of the guideline where a hook had been seated in the rock. There he secured the secondary line from the reel at his waist and scanned the mammoth cavern with his light. Joel could appreciate the visual rewards of cave diving, taking in the stunning beauty of the underwater landscape.

The agreed-upon signal for return was simply a tap on the shoulder and an upward point, but Joel was far from return ready. He had been searching, scanning as he went, from the start. When Phillip looked around with a questioning gesture, Joel pointed ahead to the other side of the great room where the passage continued. Phillip nodded and swam on, trailing the new guideline. With the many turns and portals along the way, it would be the only sure way of return when the time came.

They were past the limit of most cave dives which was 130 feet. With increasing depth Joel noticed more of a salty taste to the water which indicated a link to the sea, along with more pressure on his ears and more difficulty in breathing. Slowly they kept going through narrowing and expanding tunnels.

Eventually they reached the end of Phillip's guideline. He lifted his hands and looked at Joel, still searching with his light. The gradually descending cavern floor had leveled off and there was a vertical drop ahead. Joel had come this far and had to see what was down there even though it meant releasing the line.

Phillip saw Joel heading for the hole and motioned for him to come back, but it was pointless. Too much was at stake to give up before looking at one last unexplored level. Straight down he went, sweeping the gigantic pillared walls and rocky bottom with his light, an estimated 75 feet deeper. Something below among the rocks was reflecting his beam—it was pale white, like bones.

As Joel swam further down, the object became recognizable—the skeletal remains of a giant serpent that stretched along the rocks over thirty feet, ending at a large triangular head. Incredible. Like nothing he had ever seen, perhaps from an era long ago.

His attention was interrupted by a light from above. There at the rim was Simon, waving and calling his name through the water, "Joooeeel."

It was then that he looked around, following Simon's beam of light into an even lower darkness, to an opening between the columns on the opposite side of the pit. He redirected his own light in the same direction. Something massive was moving, churning the dark lower waters with clouds of sediment. Shifting shadows were coming fast in his direction.

Fear of the unknown is common to man, instilled for a purpose that God's image-bearers might run to Him for deliverance. Joel knew this inwardly, but he felt more petrified than the bone he was hoping to find. It was too late to move.

At the leading edge of the cloud, there were shapes that he first thought to be large fish. But they soon revealed upper bodies like men. There was no time to swim away. Within a minute they were upon him, moving swiftly with powerful tails like dolphins.

Those nearest pulled a rope net which was quickly over and around him. After dropping his light, Joel could see no more. There was only the squeeze of the netting and the frightening sensation of being rushed through the waters.

From above for Simon, the scene was surreal. With his light from the rim of the drop-off, he witnessed the storm of strange creatures advancing upon Joel, wrapping him with a net, and carrying him away. He felt powerless to help his friend. Neither he nor Phillip who had come alongside could do anything.

About to swim down, Simon was halted by the sight of two creatures coming up toward them. They had seen his light. He had no weapon but a small knife in a case on his belt and no time to remove it. Phillip was in the same fix.

He kept his light on them as they rapidly approached thinking that it might turn them away, but it didn't. Propelled by their powerful tails, the grim-faced mermen covered the distance in seconds. The diver's light was knocked from his grip and sent tumbling into the pit. There was nothing else to see or grab. All was dark.

Suddenly he was struck on his side and pushed against the rocky floor by the creature he could no longer see.

Simon turned and twisted to no avail. The thing had hold on him from behind. His head jerked back with the pull against his regulator hoses and the shocking sound of air rapidly escaping from his tanks. Like a trained assassin, the creature had found the most vulnerable place to attack.

As quickly as they had come, they were gone, leaving Simon floundering with no air supply. He was able to take half a breath before coughing, the water already invading the tubes. With the realization that he might be about to drown, Simon put his desperate thoughts on the One who held the keys to life, the One with power to part the sea– Jesus. If this was the time, Simon was ready to join his Savior. The air in his lungs wouldn't last long.

A flash of light. Then a steady beam. It was Phillip coming toward him pointing to Simon's waist, the nylon holster that held his bail-out bottle. With Phillip's help, the mini-air-cylinder was removed and quickly deployed.

The fresh oxygen sent a wave of relief to Simon's system. He was thankful to still be alive. Phillip was also using his small back-up tank as both of their air hoses had been ripped loose sending bubbles streaming upward.

With the bubbles hitting the cavern ceiling, sediment began falling. Seeing this, Phillip motioned for a hasty return while picking up the guideline.

There was no choice. They had to leave to stay alive. Once out of the Guardian, they could try to sort things out and decide what to do next, about Joel.

16

Below 130 feet is considered beyond the scope of recreational diving. Nitrogen narcosis, also referred to as raptures of the deep, usually hits divers at such depths. Except for helium and neon, all gases that can be breathed have a narcotic effect with increasing pressure.

Joel had been briefed on this and was feeling no pain from the tight rope netting. He didn't care what was happening to him, in fact felt like laughing at the strange way he was being escorted through the water by mermaids, mermen, or whatever they were. He was in a comic book.

They had passed through cavernous tunnels lined with dagger-like stalactites. The macabre black-green surroundings of the Guardian's lower portals had been chilling, but now it didn't matter. He was giddy. Was this how a dying drunk man felt on his initial descent into Hades? Did Jonah laugh as he was swallowed? That he doubted.

A faint light from far above allowed Joel to see as the fish people departed the tunnel system into what appeared to be the main ocean plunging even deeper. His euphoria was being overtaken with a dizziness and overall numbness at the greater pressure depth. His ears felt like they would burst. He was being gripped with the netting by the creatures at his sides and watched their shadowy movement, the up and down push of their huge tails, their lengths estimated at nine to twelve feet. The faces he preferred not to see, as an earlier glimpse before he lost his light revealed a wolverine countenance with threatening teeth.

Joel was beginning to sense a detachment from his body, a helplessness to escape his pressure wrap that was close to engulfing him. Just as he was near to losing consciousness, he was twisted out of the netting and pushed into a long casket-shaped container. The lid closed, sealing him in total darkness. All he wanted to think was Jesus.

"What time was it when the three of you began your dive?" Andros Police Captain Austin, with pen in hand and a tired expression, spoke across his office desk to the two divers seated in unfolded aluminum chairs.

"Close to ten this morning," said Phillip.

"You've been doing this awhile?"

"Five years as a master diver."

"And you've never lost a diver before?"

"Never. Others have. Six this year, in our area."

The Captain frowned, looking at a plaque on an otherwise bare plaster wall. "Terrible for tourism."

Phillip had called the police as soon as they had left the blue hole, to report a missing diver, then had driven to the station where Simon attempted to describe the details of what he had seen.

"Is there a search and rescue team around here?" Simon asked, perplexed at the lack of responsiveness.

Austin was taking his time filling out the paperwork. "Mister Simon Johnson. Correct?"

"That's right."

"And your visiting friend, Joel—"

"Landon. L-a-n-d-o-n, the one who was taken."

"Yes, by the mermaids."

"Mermen."

"I stand corrected. As you say, mermen."

"How am I supposed to describe them, with tails like fish and upper bodies like men?"

"Maybe they were frogmen." The Captain had a stupid grin on his face. "Who knows, the Russians have been prowling around lately."

"Fine, but they had no air tanks."

"Okay. Phillip, did you see these things?"

"Not exactly."

"Either you did, or you didn't."

"There was a lot of sediment stirred up by something. Too cloudy to see clearly."

"Two of them came up from below and tore our air hoses," said Simon.

"You did not see them?" asked the Captain looking at Phillip.

"The lights were dropped," said Phillip.

"So, Mister Johnson was the only one who actually saw these supposed mermen." It was not a question.

Simon and Phillip looked at each other without reply.

"Your recorded depth was below 130 feet. Correct?"

"Yes," said Phillip.

"The secondary guideline had run out?"

"Yes."

"You are aware as a master diver that hallucinations can occur at such depths."

"What I saw, Sir," said Simon, "was not any hallucination."

"I am sure it was very real to you," said the Captain, laying his pencil down, "and I wish to express my sympathy for the loss of your friend."

"What about our ripped air hoses? How do you explain that?" said Simon.

"Of course. Our caverns are filled with stalactites and other protrusions which can easily snag and tear loose an air hose." Austin got up from his seat and extended a hand. "I wish there was something more I could do."

There was nothing more that Simon and Phillip could do but to return to Small Hope Lodge.

The lid of Joel's casket slowly lifted. The water had drained out and a three-fingered hand appeared on the edge. Then a face almost human, with a snout like a pig and a shiny head. There were two of them looking down at him.

He allowed himself to be lifted, his gear removed, and to be seated on an upright metal gurney by the pig people.

"Where am I?"

Joel's question was left hanging in the windowless room as the two busied themselves with adjustments and straps, securing him to the wheeled contraption.

With grunts and searching eyes they made their way around a central pool of water which was rapidly disappearing beneath the closed transport box. The only sound was the whine of a vacuum which ended as the last of the water flushed out.

After giving attention to a wall-mounted control panel, the pot-bellied duo returned to the gurney and adjusted the back with about ten degrees more tilt for Joel's comfort. Their little grins were unnerving, as though their intentions could be benevolent. With wistful blue eyes they stared for a moment, communicating what seemed to Joel an inner sadness. Joel would've been sad too, he thought, if he woke up part pig. In their zippered white uniforms, they could have almost passed for humans.

"Do you guys speak?"

Although there was no audible reply, Joel took note of the way they looked at each other, as though they understood his question but were mutually agreed to a code of silence. At this point they turned and exited the room through an automated doorway.

Joel sat in silent constraint for at least an hour pondering his predicament. What was this place beneath the sea? How did all these strange creatures come to be? And what did they want with him?

"And whose great mind is behind it?" The mind-reading voice was disarmingly familiar.

As the door slid open, Joel saw the one he had suspected was behind all his problems.

"What's the matter my little reporter? Cat got your tongue?" Just the sight of his helpless, dripping captive strapped and delivered to him was tantalizing to Lucas. The chase was over. Finally, here was the soul who refused to go away and be silenced, the mite who had brought embarrassment to him in the presence of the rulers.

"Pride goes before a fall," said Joel, figuring he didn't have anything to lose by speaking truth.

"Testy words for a man who could soon be a rat in a genetic laboratory, along with your female companion."

"You have Amber, here?"

"Jo-el Landon. You have been nothing but an annoying flea."

"Guess I hopped on a dog."

"Far from it, my unfortunate fellow. Your nose for news has brought you into the mouth of the beast."

"Frankly I don't see anything much going on here but a few pig people."

"Just one of our start-up transgenic experiments, surprisingly intelligent. I'm glad to see you found the tritons, or should I say they found you."

"So, mer-people are your doing?"

"They started long before my time, or did you study that?"

"Sure, taught as legends and mythology."

"Like many other forms we are duplicating, originally seeded by the gods."

"Seeding doesn't explain life's origin. It only pushes the Creation further away."

"Don't tell me you claim to be a scientist."

"I don't need to be. My Creator has written how it all got here, including the transgenic forms, a corruption of God's creation by the fallen angels."

"You shouldn't be speaking of things you know nothing about."

"Were you there?"

"Where?"

"On Mount Hermon, before the flood, in the days of Jared." Simon had shared with him that revelation of Genesis 6 from the writings of Enoch.

"Enough my small-minded reporter. I ask the questions here."

Silence.

"You would see how little you know, if I chose to show you around."

Silence.

It bothered Lucas that this peanut brain reporter acted like he knew more than him. The more he thought about it, he decided, like the cat, to play with the mouse before eating it. He telepathically summoned one of his orderlies. Lucas would allow this young upstart to see some of his incredible accomplishments, just to gloat a little, like prodding the rodent to see how he wiggled. Soon one of the transgenics arrived.

"Alf, we're going to give our captive visitor a tour before disposition."

"With a short grunt of understanding, the pig-man orderly took hold of Joel's gurney, released the wheel locks, and pushed.

Lucas led the way through the fossil museum, pausing briefly at each exhibit to observe the expression on Joel's face. As with the Jesuit, the surprised look grew with each stop. He kept the description short, not so interested in educating as in shocking his captive's shallow worldview. Vengeance came in many ways.

The bone museum had been his brain-child, a tool of indoctrination which had proven useful in securing cooperation from the world's shadow-governing heads.

Moving from the giant, past the skeletal reconstructions of the equestrian and avian hybrids, their final pause was in front of the triton.

"Look familiar?" Alf turned the gurney so that Joel was facing the structure.

Joel was silently taking it in.

"Thanks to a veterinarian's inquiry from Green Port, we secured this addition to our collection. As you can see, the jawbone is re-attached."

"A lot of trouble for a pile of bones."

"Bones kept from prying eyes."

"Why keep it so hidden?"

"As the scientist and philosopher, Francis Bacon, said, 'knowledge is power'."

"You're hiding the truth of earth's history."

"Controlling it for a better future."

Silence.

"I recall an interview I once had with a small-town reporter." Pause. "Very curious he was."

"Yeah, you kicked me out."

"Your questions were foolish."

"Any fool should know that big bangs don't produce order, much less life."

Lucas was growing annoyed when his message signal sounded. His presence was needed in the lab.

"Alf, give our skeptical visitor a glimpse of the other side. I'll meet you both afterwards in the transit room."

There he would give the order for Joel's disposition. A feeding seemed appropriate.

17

Alf spoke slowly in a husky voice which came as a surprise to Joel, having heard no words from either of the pig people since being portaled into the deep-sea base. "It is better not to speak. Just look."

The long passageway reminded him of an airline terminal through which they were hurrying to make a connecting flight, though he had trouble imagining a departing flight on the "other side" as they called it.

They passed through two sets of doorways, the first opening automatically, the second requiring biometric identification from Alf's three-fingered hand. As they neared the end, Joel tensed at the sight of what stood before them. The creature was like a man with scales for skin, standing as a sentry, scrutinizing the visitor on wheels. Alf strutted around and up to it, reached out and dropped something shiny into its hand, then stepped back to the gurney. The reptilian stepped to the side and waved them on into a narrow hallway.

"Nasty things," said Alf, "always wanting to be paid for doing nothing."

Soon they came to a silvery wall that shimmered like liquid. Alf kept rolling him forward without slowing. "Where are we going?" said Joel.

"Don't talk. We are entering their side."

Joel tried to turn his legs away but couldn't. His feet went first into the wall, disappearing, then the rest of his body, sliding through the cold silvery curtain. He reactively closed his eyes. When they reopened, he found himself at the edge of a massive workplace the size of a football field which housed spherical metallic objects all glowing with pale blue phosphorescence. Still in his gurney with Alf also fully inside, Joel tried to process all that he was seeing but with great difficulty.

He didn't believe in this stuff—flying saucers and little gray men. Yes, he was observing them, but they couldn't be real, any more than the lizard men or pig people. He blinked, wondering, hoping that it all might go away, but no. Strange little beings walked around with over-sized heads and dark almond-shaped eyes, entering and exiting the various craft, some hovering, some sitting. It had to be a movie set. Please, let it be. Joel blinked again.

One wandered toward him, checking out this different species in their area. Joel's uneasiness increased the closer it came. Big black eyes. No real expression. Benevolent? Who knows? Now less than ten feet away with a cute little mouth, was he trying to grin? To make friends?

"Jesus," whispered Joel, reactively.

Instantly, the little fellow sprang back, his face contorted with the most hateful look Joel had ever seen. A set of viper teeth protruded from the corners of his mouth along with a protracted "Hissss". It crouched and narrowed its eyes while keeping its distance.

Joel felt the gurney move. Quickly it swung around and was shoved back into and through the silvery wall. "I said not to talk," said Alf. "You made them angry."

"How? It was barely a whisper."

"You must be very careful." Alf huffed as he sped the gurney back through the passageway, past the scaly sentinel and the doorways, returning to the side from which they had come.

Restrained in a glass bubble, inside a steel-walled circular room, housing other bubble occupants with strange looking examiners and supervisors coming and going, Amber couldn't have been more disoriented. Adding to her confusion was a faint perception she had received while gazing through a hall doorway which had been left open.

So ridiculous was the vision that she wanted to laugh, but it rolled through the hallway too fast to study—a man with the snout of a pig, pushing another man in a rolling chair. If she could only have gotten a second look. Funny but sad, how the one reminded her of Joel. Her mind was playing tricks.

At least it temporarily helped to keep her from thinking about the instrument cart that had been moved alongside her, signaling that it was her time. Intravenous tubes and monitors had been connected to her following the overseer's frustration with Amber's lack of cooperativeness. She was slowly drifting into a drug-induced dream state while hearing the far-eastern wail of pipe and flute music within her bubble.

Until now, sheer will power had worked to forestall the intrusion she had watched others painfully endure—the shrieks and convulsions that accompanied ovarian harvesting and implants.

Joel grimaced from the *slap* of Lucas's hand to the side of his face. Alf 's snout quivered as he backed away from the gurney. The Doctor was livid, pacing back and forth in the transit room. Whatever it was Joel had done must have been the final straw.

"Worthless worm—you are like an invader in my world that won't quit."

Joel gazed back through half-opened eyes without reply.

"You have embarrassed me for the last time. Alf should never have given you a glimpse of the other side."

Silence.

Lucas raised his hand for another slap, then slowly let it down. "You had to say that Name, didn't you?"

It suddenly occurred to Joel what it was, as he remembered how the alien had reacted. "You mean the Name of J–"

"Silence!" The hand recoiled and swung again with a slap. Alf cringed in the doorway. "If you had only been a good little reporter, minding your own business, you could have married what's-her-name and lived out your lives like normal people."

"What have you done with Amber?"

"If I were to tell you, your small mind couldn't begin to fathom the cooperative agenda, much less appreciate the rise and rule of the universal head."

"The only Head I know is Je– "

"Shut up, you idiot. Not that Name, which is never to be spoken here below. That Bible of yours-every copy should be destroyed."

"People have tried."

Lucas leveled his finger at Joel. "If you had simply kept your religion to yourself, you might have lived a long and prosperous life."

"What do you know about life?"

"With your DNA fixed, like mine, it could have gone on indefinitely. But unfortunately for you, you won't live to see tomorrow."

"You can't take my life. It's been given to Jesus."

The expression of prideful annoyance on the Doctor's face immediately changed to resolute rage. Turning to Alf he said, "Feed him to Gorzon."

"Welcome to our Island House of Prayer, Phillip. Who is your friend?" The white-haired elder got up from his bench to greet the two men approaching through the darkness. A naked porch bulb provided recognition.

"His name is Simon," said Phillip, taking the smiling islander's hand. "Simon, meet James."

The sound of singing could be heard from inside, an old favorite hymn. It was Amazing Grace, coming from a harmonious group of voices.

"Hope we're not too late," said Simon.

"No way, my friend. We are here for as long as you need. Welcome, and come in."

Inside the Andros bungalow, five natives sat and sang, immersed in their hymn worship. After the ending chorus, they turned their attention to the new arrivals. Introductions were made around the room and all made Simon feel like family.

"Our brother, what is it you need the good Lord to do in your life?" said one of the men looking at Simon.

"It is not so much for me as for another brother in the Lord who is missing—"

"From a deep dive in the Guardian," said Phillip, finishing Simon's reply. "I guided them down."

"If he drowned, we are very sorry."

"Joel was seized," said Simon. "I saw him being taken away through a lower cavern."

"By the tritons?" said James.

"You know of them?" said Phillip.

"Our fathers told us of them. There is much devilish activity in the history of our island."

"Then you believe me?" said Simon.

"Of course, we know it is true. We must pray fervently for your friend."

"And his female friend, Amber," said Phillip. "He was searching for her."

Just then, an older woman lifted her hands and boldly stated, "They are both alive but in great danger. The Lord has given me a vision. We must intercede for them without delay."

The circle of believers together fell to their knees with Simon and Phillip. There was no hesitation. They were being led by the One Holy Spirit. The power Simon felt was reassuring as different ones voiced their prayers and the group signaled unified agreement.

Simon had sensed the presence of God from the moment he had stepped into the room. He knew the Lord inhabited the praises of His people, as promised in His Word. Now, through the warfare of faith they were taking hold of other promises and declaring the words of authority from the throne of Jesus Christ to the underlying powers of darkness, the principalities and rulers, for protection and deliverance.

There was no doubt in Simon's mind that God had brought him here. It was a powerhouse of prayer warriors greater than anything he had witnessed at home. Perhaps there were others like them. There needed to be. The heavens had opened. He was unconscious of the time it was taking, pressing in through intercession until at last there was a release sensed in his spirit and a supernatural peace. Their prayers were being answered. There was great faith in the house.

Some were now standing, others sitting, all with bright and peaceful countenances. James gave Phillip a hug with the words, "We want to see you back soon. Don't wait for an emergency."

"I'll be back," said Phillip.

"You're also welcome anytime," said James to Simon.

"I've met my Andros family," said Simon. The love he had witnessed was beyond anything the world had to offer.

Back in his cabin at Small Hope Lodge, Simon located a phone number for the State Capitol of Florida in Tallahassee, punched it in and waited. The operator was polite but unhelpful, until he stressed that it was a family emergency involving Senator Landon's son. She then transferred him to a private line.

"Hello."

"Is this Senator Landon?"

"Yes. Who is speaking?"

"My name is Simon Johnson."

"Do I know you?"

"We've never met, but I have news of your son. He is in great danger."

"Is this some kind of ransom notice? If it is, you can keep him."

"Not at all, but I'm sorry that you feel that way."

"What do you want?"

"Joel needs your help."

"Finding a sea cow?"

"Far more than that."

"What's your connection and, where is he?"

"I'm a chaplain in Green Port, but I'm calling from Andros Island in the Bahamas."

"The boy needs psychiatric help. We had to put him in an institution."

"The whole thing was a conspired set-up. Your son's not crazy."

"I hope that you can back up what you are saying."

"Please allow me a few minutes and I'll do my best to explain."

"Go ahead."

Simon prayerfully unfolded the situation.

Following Simon's lengthy conversation with Senator Landon, he sat down and tried calling Captain Ron.

There was no answer, so he sent a text, "If still in area, in desperate need of your help."

18

Joel lay still, very still.

The odor was like damp cement with something dead mixed in. It was a walled pen about fifteen-feet square where Alf had dumped him before exiting through the feeding door. In Joel's past experience, the things he feared were never as bad as the fear itself, but what he was now about to face might prove to be the exception. Lucas called the thing Gorzon. Alf called it a lower portal release, whatever that meant.

In the containment area, Joel's eyes slowly adjusted to the darkness. No threats were visible inside the walls. He felt some relief.

Slowly, cautiously, he inched ahead on his knees and elbows. The hard floor was prickly with straw, as if intended for farm animals. Something stirring to his right startled him. He turned to try to focus in the dark. "Baaa," came the bleat of a small goat as it raised up, repositioned itself and lay back down.

Joel continued crawling to the wall farthest from the door. His intent was to look over it, into the larger open area behind, with hope of finding another way out. There might not be, but he wasn't going to lie around waiting to die. Others might, but he preferred to take a chance and keep moving.

Where was Amber? What was happening to her? Had they destroyed her mind? Questions dug deep into his soul adding purpose and motivation to his struggle for survival.

If he did escape and find her, how would he ever save her from their sea-bottom prison? It looked impossible.

His hands slid up the six-foot wall, fingers clutching the top. Just as he was about to peek over the edge, he froze. A scraping sound like a leathery weight being dragged, gets louder, coming closer. He doesn't know whether to look or let go. His heart is pounding.

Suddenly his fingers release the ledge, his knees buckle, and Joel sinks to the floor. He didn't have to peek over. Something out of his worst nightmare had arisen from the other side and was looking down at him.

Twenty feet tall, it sways back and forth, with three sets of arms grappling from a huge serpentine body. Its head is like a Cyclops with tusks protruding upward from the corners of its mouth. The horrendous eye in the center of its head shifts, scrutinizing its prey as its upper body swings over its food pen.

For Joel there is no place to go. Like a crab scurrying to hide behind rocks, he pushes himself into a corner, hoping beyond hope for escape.

Gorzon is ready to strike, ready to seize, ready to devour—now swinging in circles over its prize as if playing with it before taking it. Its gaze is on Joel as it moves in and out with the hypnotic movement of a cobra. The paralysis of fear is felt, squeezing against the corner wall with nowhere to turn, watching, waiting, anticipating the end at any moment.

"Jesus." Does He hear? Does He see?

Suddenly the serpent trunk came down and Joel felt the claw-like hands take hold of his legs, dragging him away from the corner. As he squirms and struggles desperately to get free, other claws grab his arms and lift him bodily like an ear of corn.

Gorzon's terrifying face with its exploring eye was close enough to kick, but such a tactic was useless in the powerful grip of six hands that stretched him and turned him while still swaying over the pen.

The wide nostrils brushed Joel's back and took a sniff. Then slowly rolling him, Gorzon's cavernous mouth opened and everything went black. Before being eaten, Joel heard one last sound from below–"Baaa."

Leaning back in his soft leather recliner, Lucas watched the scene unfold on his wall monitor within his private office while sipping on a glass of his favorite scotch whiskey. As he had eagerly expected, Gorzon found Joel in his feeding pen and was lifting him to his mouth while turning and pulling him. The gory anticipation made the Doctor drool with excitement.

Then, just as the big eye homed in and the monstrous teeth were about to sink in, ending his prolonged source of irritation, the display screen went blank–"a cursed power failure."

Hastily, Lucas summoned Ebo, one of the pig-teks (he refrained from calling them that) and issued orders for an immediate site check. Diagnostics and repairs were Ebo's specialty. Gulping from his glass, the Doctor waited and watched for the screen picture to recover, despising the interruption.

At last the image of Gorzon returned, with his mouth closed. Its trunk with multiple arms was undulating and a bulge was evident moving slowly downward as serpents do with their food following ingestion. Downing the last of his drink, Lucas sat up and turned off the monitor. He grinned with delight, relieved that his blight had been removed. Joel Landon would bother him no more.

As for Joel's father, the State Senator, that problem too would soon pass after hearing of his son's disappearance and later drowning during a blue-hole dive, which was not uncommon in the area. As for the girlfriend, she had no family, no one who cared. They would keep using her as a host for their continuing transgenic work. Everything was fixed and neatly in place. No more loose ends.

Lucas picked up the secure phone and punched the code for the Endor Master of Operations.

"What is it, Lucas?"

"You will be pleased to hear the news."

"You're thinking of leaving?" Lucas hated their attempt at humor.

"I am calling to report all threats of security compromise eliminated."

Silence.

"Did you hear what I just reported?"

"Carry on, Lucas. Your work is under review."

Their ways of watching disturbed him. His right hand had developed a tremble.

Joel's body was sore, but it could have been broken after dropping ten feet in the dark. Thankfully, a clump of straw had cushioned the impact. He had reacted instinctively after the fall by quickly shuffling away from the inside wall to the corner closest to the outside feeding door through which he had been dumped.

Instead of him, the goat was gone, and the hybrid serpent was out of sight behind the wall. In the dim light Joel could see that the pen was empty, no food remaining except himself. Miraculously he was still alive, but how much longer? How soon would he hear the scraping movement and see the looming shape of the serpentine Cyclops returning for another meal?

For now, there was dead silence, nothing Joel sensed but the musky serpent and straw odor. All he could do was wait, try to be calm, and recover.

19

Barely a minute had passed when the "click" of the door mechanism caused Joel to sit up. It opened slowly. A face appeared in the crack, then a three-fingered hand. It was Alf motioning for him to come out of the pen. Joel scuttled through the doorway to where Alf and Ebo were waiting, outside Gorzon's feed door.

"We came expecting to find an empty pen," said Ebo, eyes wide with amazement.

"Your God must be strong. We want no trouble," said Alf, "so we help you get out."

Joel looked around. The gurney was next to a wall. "That thing again?"

"Leave it," said Alf.

The escape was welcome, but not without Amber. "My God would not be happy if I was the only one to go." They looked at him strangely. "There is a young lady who must go with me."

Before they could respond, a jolting *thud* shook the feed room and swung the door wide. An ugly head with an eye appeared–Gorzon! The feeding door had not been secured.

Alf darted through the outer doorway pulling on the arm of Joel who was trying to move fast with Ebo pushing from behind and slamming the second door closed.

"Will it hold?" asked Joel, following Alf 's lead through the main passageway.

"We won't wait to see," said Ebo.

Amber flinched and opened her eyes at the cold probe by the creature against her flesh. She was still semiconscious from the drugs dripping through the tubes into her bloodstream. The bubble covering to her container had been removed and the medical cart was ready.

Three humanoid shapes were standing in front of her—a tall reptilian with two short grays wearing surgical masks, like cartoon animals. But she was in no mood for amusement, especially seeing what they were preparing to do. She had watched with horror as it happened to others in the room. One gray was adjusting the tilt. The other was inspecting instruments, while the scaly one prepared the syringe. The unthinkable was proceeding.

She prayed in desperation to a God she didn't really know, unable to fathom the existence of such evil. Helpless confusion surrounded her mind in this place in which she was held against her will by beings so strange and foreign. Maybe it was all a bad dream and she would wake up on the floor, having fallen out of her bed, as she once did as a child. How she wished it would all be over.

"Amber?" The human voice was Joel's. She had to be dreaming.

The three creatures suddenly dropped what they were holding and turned to the open doorway where a man stood.

"Amber!" It was Joel, along with two others with pig-like noses.

She tried to respond but her voice was gone, and her arms were restrained.

Joel headed in her direction, but a gray jumped in his way. Not about to be blocked, he drew back with his fist and threw a hard punch to the gray's surgical mask. Amber wanted to clap as the force of Joel's hit lifted the gray up and sent him sprawling across the room.

The other gray backed off but the reptilian advanced toward Joel. As Joel prepared to fight, the creature pointed a finger at him. Suddenly, an invisible force lifted him in the air like an actor suspended by wires. He dangled in mid-air. Then with a forward thrust of the reptilian's hand, the force sent Joel flying against the wall where he collapsed to the floor. No others dared to move.

"Lord Jesus, help us," Amber heard herself say. Before her next breath there was an explosive flash of light and a shriek from the reptilian.

In the center of the room appeared a man—no—an angel in radiant white whose stature reached the ceiling, dressed as a warrior, a double-edged sword in his hand. His countenance was frightening yet reassuring that help had arrived.

On the floor, with fingers still twitching, was the severed forearm of the reptilian who was clutching the stub that remained and backing away from the glory light.

Then Amber heard a sound—a *"swoosh"*, and saw the sudden manifestation of a second man, somewhat smaller and darker than the first. The two faced one another as foes.

"What brings you to my region, Michael?" said the dark one.

"Only for a little longer, Atlantis. You've had your glory."

"It will return."

"By deception. Then your end will come."

"You haven't answered me," said Atlantis.

"Two of these belong to Y'SHUA," said the tall warrior angel.

"We have legal rights to these dirt bags."

"They have called on His Name."

Atlantis drew his sword. "You can't have them."

"Are you that foolish?" Michael lifted his sword ablaze with glory fire.

Atlantis stood angry and defiant.

"I won't speak to you again," said Michael. "Stand down or you will perish on this spot."

The dark one slowly sheathed his weapon, and then vanished.

Michael turned to Joel who was standing, recovered from his encounter. "Go. Loose your friend and leave this cursed place."

The reptilian had backed far away, still nursing what was left of his arm. The grays were gone. Michael remained, his luminescence filling the room until Joel, with the help of Alf and Ebo, disconnected all the tubes and restraining ties on Amber's body.

When Joel looked into her eyes, the inexpressible connection he felt made everything worthwhile. He placed his arm around her to lift her from the bubble. She responded by placing both of her arms around his neck and drawing close. Although she was weak from her lengthy confinement, Amber struggled with all the energy she had and managed to get on her feet.

Michael vanished as Ebo led the way out through the door. With Joel on one side and Alf on the other, Amber hobbled as quickly as she could through the corridor.

"How do we get out?" said Joel.

"The sea portal," said Ebo, looking back to make sure the others were keeping up.

"The same way I came in?"

"Yes, not the way she did," said Alf.

"How did Amber arrive?"

"From the other side."

"A UFO portal?"

"USO–submersible," said Alf.

"How much further?" said Amber. "How can we get out?"

Just then, an ear-splitting sound like repeated blasts on an air horn began to echo through the passageway and red lights started flashing.

"It's a security breach," said Ebo, yelling back. "Hurry."

"The entrance is just ahead," said Alf, puffing.

Joel saw the doorway growing narrower as the sliding door was slowly closing.

"It's a system lock-down," said Ebo. "Move inside fast."

With a burst of effort, all four squeezed through just as the steel door slid shut and locked.

Joel looked around. It was the room he remembered, the place he had entered Endor from the sea. In the center of the floor was a partially full trough of water and transport box. It looked like a giant projectile waiting to slide into the discharge chamber.

Alf and Ebo went first to the box, opening the lid. Ebo then went to the control settings, making the necessary adjustments. Alf motioned for Joel and Amber to come and get in.

"It looks like a casket," said Amber, stepping down to the side with Joel's help. "You sure it's safe?"

"It only needs to take you up," said Alf.

The box was just wide enough for both of them, but cozy. "Where are the controls?" Joel asked, easing himself in alongside Amber.

"You have none," said Alf. "Everything is preset for a gradual ascent."

"We just float to the surface?"

"Unless the tritons interfere. With the security breach, they should be somewhere else."

"Is there enough air in here?"

"Everything is charged and regulated."

"Guess we're good to go," said Joel, managing a smile. Amber had a hopeful expression. "Thanks for helping us, Alf and Ebo. Can't you guys get away too?" Joel spotted another box.

"We will probably die, either way," said Alf, meeting eyes with Ebo. "At least here we can find ways to slow down the plans of their false gods."

Joel and Amber were silent.

"Remember us when you speak to your God," said Ebo.

Joel was about to reply when the lid to the box closed with a vacuum sound. The two of them were sealed, in absolute darkness, side by side. They heard the outside water level rising and felt the shift as the box moved. Mechanical noises. Small holding doors, opening and closing.

After a brief pause, the box jettisoned forward free from all constraints. No more sounds.

"It feels like we're floating," said Amber. "Hopefully rising," said Joel.

"Have we really escaped?" "Pray."

"I haven't stopped."

Simon sat at the end of the dock at Small Hope Bay, his feet dangling in the water, watching a speck on the horizon get larger and take shape. It was a fast boat with a rooster tail of spray being kicked up from behind. Soon the deep whine of its powerhouse was audible and the red stripe on its bow was visible.

Captain Ron had responded like a true Navy Seal to Simon's call for assistance. They had a long friendship and had helped each other in various ways over the years. Fortunately, Ron was still in the area and liked getting involved in strategic missions.

Simon caught the line as Ron maneuvered the long rumbling craft alongside the dock.

"A different boat," said Simon.

"Yep, made a trade." Captain Ron had been a dealmaker with boats as long as Simon had known him. "Fifty-foot Maurauder. More room and just as fast."

"Will you ever give up these cigarettes?"

"Never going back to the kind that kill. What's up and where's Joel?"

"Let's grab a cup of java and I'll fill you in."

After securing the boat, the two men walked to the nearby Bay Café where they sat down, prayed for God's help, and took time to discuss a plan of action.

"Just being honest," said Ron, "if I wasn't a man of faith, I wouldn't give your friend the chance of a snowball in hell, being alive."

"That's why I called you."

"Well, we can do a search if you know where to look."

Simon spread a nautical chart out on the table that showed the depths and contour of the ocean off Andros Island. "It's this area I believe we need to search. The Tongue of The Ocean."

"Six thousand feet down," said Ron, taking a closer look. "No telling what might come out of there."

"How long do you think it'll take to cover the area?"

"We can do a grid search in half a day and make use of surface radar."

"You came equipped."

"All the bells and whistles, and fast as a Coast Guard chopper."

"Let's do it. Need any drinks?" said Simon, rolling up the chart.

"Already got a full cooler."

Soon the two returned to the boat and got underway heading out to the GPS coordinates Ron had set up for the grid. The weather was fair, and the offshore surface was smooth, ideal conditions for a search.

"Any idea what we're looking for, other than a head in the water?" said Captain Ron, pushing on the twin throttles.

"Not really sure. Maybe a flotation device."

"Okay, there's a pair of binoculars in the console."

Simon picked them up and settled back against the port bolster seat. Standing gave him a better vantage point. After setting the course on the autopilot, Ron opened a bottle of water and turned on the radar.

As the morning passed, they worked through half the grid, then slowed briefly for a snack before resuming speed. Simon was getting weary and concerned that he might have missed seeing Joel, struggling to stay afloat, maybe clinging to a board barely visible. He tried to stay in the place of faith but felt himself slipping, then tried to recall some of the Scriptural promises that had been spoken at the Island House prayer meeting.

Neither man spoke much for a couple of hours, realizing their search was about over and they had not seen a thing. The last leg of the grid took them back toward Andros.

"Not sure where else to look, friend," said Ron. "Nothing to report on radar but another boat."

"Let's check 'em out. Maybe they have seen something," said Simon.

As they got within sight of the other larger boat, Simon was surprised to see Ron reach under the controls and pull out a military-type rifle.

"What's up?"

"Rotten salvage pirates. I recognize the boat. Be ready to hit the deck if I tell you."

Simon would have welcomed a little excitement after half a day of disappointment, but this was over the top. *Okay, Lord, whatever you have.*

The floating rig they were approaching looked like it had been pieced together from a junkyard—a boarded wood hull, metal sheets tacked to the wheelhouse, and a long barge-like open deck piled with junk. It was noisy and belched smoke from a vertical pipe.

As they got within a hundred feet, two men emerged, one holding a handgun, the other with a portable megaphone. Captain Ron waved without concealing his weapon. The man with the loudspeaker returned a weak wave and spoke between the boats.

"How's my old amigo, Captain Ron?"

Leaning into the dash-mic, Ron replied, "Same as ever, Coot." His voice bellowed from a forward speaker.

"You here on business?"

"Just business. No trouble, Coot."

"What do you need, Captain?"

"Seen or picked up anything around this area today?"

"You here to buy?"

"Could be, Coot. What you got?"

"Money first."

"How much?"

"Two hundred. Good price for what we found."

"Toss the bolo."

Simon watched as the man put down his gun and picked up a line with a weighted end. He swirled it a few times over his head, then let it soar across the water into Ron's boat.

"Got a fifty?" asked Ron. He picked up the weight and pulled in the line that was released from the other boat. A waterproof pouch was fastened to the trailing end.

"One fifty is all I've got," said Simon, digging it out of his wallet.

Ron took the bill, sealed it in the pouch and sent it back the same way.

"What are we buying?"

"Who knows, but it can't be worth more than fifty. Coot always asks too much."

The man had retrieved the bolo. Coot looked angry, then banged his fist on the bulkhead.

"What now?" said Simon.

"They'll clear us to come alongside. Help me with the fenders."

"Better wait." It appeared to Simon that the two men were sliding something across the deck from the junk pile but were not stopping with it. He watched as a long box slipped over the edge and splashed down into the sea.

Coot spoke again through the megaphone, "Fish it out, Captain. Maybe you can use a casket."

"A what?" said Simon.

The salvage boat was billowing smoke as it pulled away with its clattering engine.

"Stand by to take it aboard," said Captain Ron as he played with the twin throttles, twisting the boat alongside the floating cargo. "We paid for it. We better get it."

With the help of two boat hooks and a net, they managed to grapple the heavy box out of the sea, over the side, and onto the deck behind the seats.

"Looks pretty well sealed," said Ron. "Guess we can wait till we have time to force it open."

Simon was about to agree when he heard a thump. "Something's moving in it."

"We better go ahead and look." Ron went down into the cabin and came out with some tools. "You take the crowbar and I'll work with the hammer and chisel." For almost thirty minutes, Ron and Simon hammered and pried around the lid of the box with no success.

Finally, Simon said, "Lord, we need your help."

It was then that he noticed a small square protrusion at one end. He wondered if it would move and pushed on it. It slid an inch. Air suddenly hissed from the edge of the lid.

Amazed, Simon and Ron watched as the lid automatically lifted. They couldn't believe what they were seeing. They looked at one another, then looked again with gaping mouths.

Joel gazed up with a smile and nudged Amber with his elbow. She opened her eyes.

20

After resting most of the night in his private quarters, Doctor Lucas Redding awoke, startled by the sound of Endor's security breach alarm. He got up from his couch and went quickly to the supervisory panel where lights were flashing and activated the scanning monitor.

The active camera displayed the scene at the source of the problem—the feed room for Gorzon. The picture showed the doorway from the area looking like it had been pried open with a giant can opener.

Lucas shifted to another camera mounted in the center of the ceiling in Gorzon's chamber. A sick feeling was starting to rise as he slowly rotated the view—90 degrees, 180, 270, to 360. He viewed the full circle, every possible spot, not wanting to think of such a problem. After running through the search process twice, stopping every ten degrees, he realized Gorzon was loose.

He sat down, breathing deeply, his hand clutching the camera control, eyes fixed on the changing wall monitor. Starting at the doorway to the feeding room, Lucas transitioned cameras through the main corridor looking for signs of Gorzon's path. With his other hand, he pressed the signal button to summon his aids, wondering what happened to Alf and Ebo and why the security door had failed to hold their serpent god—their gift from the underworld.

A sensor light was on in the main lab, not far from the breach. Upon switching to the lab camera, Lucas froze.

The experimental area looked like the aftermath of an 8-point earthquake, with smashed equipment, broken vials and writhing body parts all mixed in on the floor. The condition had gone from serious to catastrophic.

Much of Endor, all the trangenetic projects, was under Lucas's responsibility. He had suddenly lost control while he was sleeping. An abdominal surge of pain added to his discomfort as the thought of Joel Landon came to mind. He was supposed to have been eaten. What had happened and where were the two he had entrusted with the feeding? Still no response. He pressed the signal button a second time.

Lucas followed the camera images from the lab entrance through the corridor, pausing along the way for a closer look at the unbelievable destruction. His mind was racing. It was a security breach. He had to act.

He had the responsibility and the authority to pull the switch, but the consequences would be irreversible. That would mean the end of their connection to AUTEC, and the start of restructure elsewhere. It was the last imaginable action to take, one he desperately wanted to avoid.

Perhaps the overseers should be called, but that would require an admission that he had failed and lacked the resources to personally take care of the situation. Lucas still had his pride.

The switch to the silver cord—Endor's connection to the upper world—was to be used only in the event of a security threat that might lead to the discovery of Endor. So far, the crisis appeared to be contained and still correctable with summoned assistance.

Another sensor light was flashing. It was the sea portal compartment. Lucas immediately activated that camera. As the image sharpened, Lucas's eyes bulged at the sight of Alf and Ebo climbing into a transport box, then lifting and closing the lid over themselves. The water was rising in the ejection trough. He then realized he had been betrayed. Had they also helped his captive escape? The anger that shot to his head made it impossible to think.

His office suddenly shook with an explosive "THUD!" The main door was bent inward. He grabbed up his secure phone, rapidly punching numbers—waiting.

Another "THUD!" There was a second protrusion of metal bending further inward. Still no answer. *Where were they?*

A third "THUD!" This time Lucas dropped the phone and backed away. Hybrid hands grappled through a metal hole, tearing and enlarging the opening with super-sized strength—the untamable offspring of fallen angel, human and serpent. Having no recourse remaining, Lucas jerked open the side drawer and with trembling hand found and withdrew the key.

A head with a single eye the size of a melon plowed itself through the door-opening with spittle dripping from its twin tusks, rising as it entered.

Less than ten feet away, Lucas inserted the key into the wall-mounted switching mechanism and turned it.

Gorzon was sliding in, expanding and engulfing the room. Like a cobra it swayed, gazing down and sizing up its prey. Lucas had to act to safeguard Endor. The gods would reward him ultimately.

He felt the fingers grab hold of his leg as he stretched for the switch. As Gorzon tore him away from the wall, Lucas flipped the switch down.

Red lights across the control panel flashed. The 2-mile transport tube, known as the silver cord, disconnected and withdrew from AUTEC on Andros Island. Security-cleared workers hastened to permanently seal and erase all evidence of an undersea opening, and orders were immediately issued for a change-of-command at the Naval base to ensure that no personnel remained at the facility having any knowledge or records of Endor.

In his spirit body, Lucas stared down at his attacker from a strange spatial location. There were no remains of his mortal body. At least the horrific pain of being eaten was over and he, Lucas Redding, still existed. The promise of one day becoming a god must have been true; for here he was, ready for his rewards.

"Lucas Redding." A Voice called his name.

"I am Lucas," he answered.

"You have ignored My Holy Book which states, it is appointed unto man once to die and after this the judgment."

"I'm like one of the gods, right?"

"There is one God who is righteous, and you are not."

"Where is the God of love and forgiveness?"

"You rejected the cross of forgiveness where I poured out My love and Holy Blood to pay for your sin-sick soul."

"Give me another chance."

"You had your chances in your lifetime. After death there are no more."

"I accomplished great things with my life."

"Without faith in Jesus Christ, all your works are as filthy rags. You have ignored the one way of salvation for which I suffered and died."

"Wait. I have connections. Father Magruder."

"Your only connections are here."

"At last. Now we'll see justice."

"As you have spoken." The Voice said no more.

Two dark figures emerged from the shadows. Lucas thought he recognized them, even tried to smile at first, until they took hold of him roughly and forced him to travel in a downward direction.

Resistance was of no use. Lucas cried out as others, reptilian in appearance, clawed and pulled on his body escorting him swiftly through a dark tunnel. Lucas cringed with a fresh and surprising dimension of pain even worse than he had felt in his mortal body.

On through lower portals they dragged Doctor Redding down into a hot flaming pit where his cries were soon lost among the cries of others, where arms reached out too late, and ultimate justice was served.

His gods had lied.

"Mister Joel Landon, please report to the officers' wardroom."

Hearing his name on the intercom, Joel rolled away from the bulkhead and lowered his feet from the bunk where he had spent the night. After a brief stop in the ship's head, he put on some fresh clothes issued from the medical locker, then climbed up the steps to the main deck. Most of the soreness was gone and he was beginning to feel somewhat rested.

His father, Senator Mark Landon, was standing just inside the wardroom door as Joel entered. He was smiling and ready with a strong hug which Joel readily returned.

"Let's put the past behind," said his dad. "We're thankful you're alive."

"Thank you for coming," said Joel. He was glad to see his father, more than he could express.

Joel looked around the officers table which was cleared for their meeting. Several were seated including Amber, appearing refreshed in a blue chambray shirt, Simon in his island attire, and Commander Davis, Executive Officer of the 210-foot Coast Guard Cutter Dauntless.

"Son," his dad whispered, "I don't know how you pulled that one out of the sea, but she impresses me. Quite a catch." The comment was in keeping with his father's style.

"I think so too." They must have been talking, Joel figured, as they sat down with the others.

"How did you find us here at Andros?" Joel quizzed his father.

"You weren't in any shape to talk yesterday, so I can tell you now. We have your friend Simon to thank for calling and filling me in on the situation with Global- Tek, and for the last location where you were seen at the dive. I decided to use one of our helicopters, then contacted the Coast Guard. They had a cutter in this area with a helo-deck. Simon can fill you in on how you were found."

"Captain Ron and I had almost given up after a thorough search off of Andros," said Simon, "when the good Lord surprised us with what looked like a casket that had been pulled from the sea by some salvage pirates. We paid fifty bucks for it. When we finally opened it, there you two were in the box. I had already contacted your father who then notified us of his location on board the Dauntless, so that's where we headed in the fast boat as soon as we found you. Ron's mission was complete, so he decided to return home."

"Everyone has been so kind," said Amber. "No-one would believe all we've been through."

"Amber has informed us of some highly controversial activities that may be going on within the Navy's AUTEC base," said the Senator, glancing at the Commander who was remaining quiet.

"More than may be, dad. I saw it first-hand. Alien transgenetic experiments, and we were the lab rats." Joel noticed the trace of skepticism in the eyes of his father.

"Whatever it was you saw, wherever you and Amber have been, I want you to know I will fully check it out," said the Senator. "I placed a call this morning to the base, requesting a visit."

"What did they say?"

"They were most cooperative. As soon as their scheduled change-of-command takes place, they will arrange a facility tour."

Fat chance of seeing Endor, thought Joel.

"Meanwhile, we can't keep the Coast Guard anchored off Andros any longer. We have room for three more passengers in the chopper and will be glad to make a beach stop in Green Port."

"Before we leave," said Simon, "let me ask the Commander how they came up with the name for this ship."

Without blinking, he replied, "Considering our reputation as the top drug-buster in the Guard, it fits. Dauntless means to persevere fearlessly. It's what we do."

As they walked out to the flight deck, Joel took note of a brass plaque on the bulkhead with the ship's motto—"Sin Miedo," which was Spanish for "Without Fear." He needed that.

Joel watched the gulls soar effortlessly through the wind currents. He stretched and smiled at Amber and Simon who both looked relaxed with a cup of coffee at the round table on his boat-house deck overlooking the beach at Green Port. "Thanks for all your help with the clean-up."

"And you two, thanks for helping me at the trailer," said Amber, while reaching down to pat the furry head of Midnight, resting at her feet.

"Thank God for good neighbors," said Simon. "Not many will take in a stray dog."

"Let's not forget Murf," said Joel. He had found his turtle near a clump of palmettos near the boathouse.

"Did you say yes to Stu?" said Amber.

"I did," said Joel. "Like my dad, he's saying, let's put the past behind."

"You enjoy writing. Now you can bring a new perspective to The Beaches News."

"I need to start subscribing," said Simon.

"I'll begin with a feature article on Amber's new business, The Pet Care Place."

"You can drop in and help when you're not writing." Amber winked.

There was a pause as the group conversation shifted.

"Maybe it's time to get Simon's thoughts on all that we've been through," said Joel. "Do you see any way that we could have been seeded by aliens?"

"It's not in the Biblical record or supported by true science. In the beginning, God created the heavens and the earth–in six days, then a day of rest. Ever wonder where the week came from?" Simon paused. "In Exodus 20:9-11, Moses was told to work six days and to rest on the seventh because that's what God did when He created every basic form of life including man. We were made in God's image from the dust of the earth."

"But we saw the aliens," said Amber. "They obviously exist."

"Demonic aberrations of God's original creation, all liars like their father, Lucifer. The fact that they usually operate in darkness, hidden from view, should be a clue."

"That explains why they recoiled with anger at the Name of Jesus," said Joel.

"Remember the Nephilim in Genesis 6:4," said Simon. It speaks of them appearing then and later also, the giant offspring and genetic engineering of fallen angels.

Verse twelve states that all flesh was corrupted. It's happening again."

"Sounds transgenic to me," said Joel.

"Like mermaids, or tritons," said Amber.

"Which the dark powers try to cover up," said Simon, "through the God-haters who control the world's philosophy, education and commerce."

"So, anything found contradicting the way the world sees things is labeled an anomaly?" said Joel.

"Generally, yes," said Simon, "and the real anomaly is the cross."

Both Joel and Amber looked at Simon with a puzzled expression.

"The real anomaly in this fallen world system is the Spirit-filled Bible believer who is joined to Jesus through His love sacrifice on the cross. He refuses to let the world shape him into its mold and lays down his life to boldly declare the way of salvation for mankind. That infuriates the ruling powers and those under their evil control, which includes this whole world system according to 1 John 5:19."

"Is that why many Christians are persecuted and put to death?" said Amber.

"A glorious future with great rewards is coming for the faithful at Christ's return, but a tragic fate for those who will not receive Jesus as their Savior. It's time to put our trust in the One who died for us and was raised from the dead, as Scripture predicted and over five-hundred eyewitnesses validated. By His blood we are set free from the strongholds of Satan, the temporary god of this world-2 Corinthians 4:4."

"I've decided to be dauntless," said Joel, "to persevere fearlessly for Jesus Christ, and I don't need a drink to do it."

"Or drugs," added Amber.

"I think you two have found it," said Simon.

"What's that?" said Joel.

"Real life."

Five months later, Joel and Amber married, with Simon officiating. The evening before, the wedding party met at the Surf Club in Green Port Beach for a dinner hosted by Senator Mark Landon.

During the meal one of the servers appeared to accidentally brush Joel's arm while removing a plate. A grunt of apology was made, and the man's face caught Joel's attention along with a curious wink. If the server had the nose of a pig, Joel thought he might have coughed up his food; but no such nose, just the faint lines of perhaps some corrective surgery. *Alf? No way.*

Joel's father was finally able to arrange a visit to AUTEC, the U.S. Navy's testing facility on Andros Island. At the Senator's request, the new commanding officer gave him a thorough tour of the base, including a brief ride in a small service elevator that had been mentioned by Joel.

Nothing was said by the Senator during the tour concerning Joel and Amber's reported experience, and nothing anomalous was observed.

ABOUT THE AUTHOR

John Lowe Owens grew up in northeast Florida in a coastal community much like Anomaly's Green Port Beach. He patrolled the offshore islands while serving in the U.S. Coast Guard on board the USCGC Dauntless and later settled in Coastal Georgia. He and his family were full-time missionaries to the former USSR. He has two published novels—*The Ninth Generation* and *Anomaly*. Explore more at www.theninthgeneration.com.